Illustrated Classics

OLIVER TWIST

Charles Dickens

ILLUSTRATED CLASSICS

OLIVER TWIST

Charles Dickens

Wonder House

(An imprint of Prakash Books)

Originally published in 1838
This abridged edition published in 2024

Wonder House

(An imprint of Prakash Books)

contact@wonderhousebooks.com

ISBN : 9789354402265

Contents

About the Book

Oliver Twist, by Charles Dickens, is the story of the life of a young orphan boy named Oliver Twist, whose entire life is contained within the streets of London, where the people are so poor and desperate that they will take any risks and show no mercy to survive.

His story begins in a workhouse elsewhere where he is being ill-treated. He runs away to London where he is introduced to a gang of thieves by the Artful Dodger. He narrowly escapes from this criminal world and finally finds himself in the hands of kind and loving people.

A gripping tale of dramatic changes of fortunes, poverty, thieves, and even murder, keeps you wondering till the end—will good triumph over evil?

Oliver Twist was adapted into a film several times. In 1948 it was shot completely in black and white and directed By David Lean. The 2005 movie was directed by Roman Polanski. In 1968 the film directed by Carol Reed was nominated for eleven Academy Awards and won six. It was also made into a British musical by Lionel Bart.

About the Author

Charles Dickens was born on February 7, 1812, in Portsea, on the southern coast of England. His first novel was *The Pickwick Papers* published in 1836. In February 1837, he began writing his second novel *Oliver Twist*, or *The Parish Boy's Progress*, under the pseudonym "Boz", in the form of monthly installments in the magazine *Bentley's Miscellany*.

Charles Dickens always saw himself as a rather serious writer. He felt that his mission in life was to speak for the poor and downtrodden. In fact, in 1852, he is said to have told one of his critics not to think of his writings as means to amuse people or having no objective.

Throughout his life, Dickens published 14 major novels, many plays, a large number of short stories, and several other books and articles. Some of his famous novels include *David Copperfield, A Tale of Two Cities* and *Great Expectations*.

In his will, the manuscripts of his major works were left to his best friend John Forster. Dickens passed away in June 1870.

Chapter 1

Where it All Began

It all began in London, England, a very long time ago. If you were an orphan or just a poor child, with no home and nowhere to go, you more often than not landed up in what is called a "workhouse". It was a public building, commonly seen in both big and small towns.

It was in one such dull and dreary place, on the outskirts of London, that a little baby was born. The mother, frail, ill and very young, had taken refuge there on a cold winter's night. The parish surgeon and Sally, a poor old nurse, were the only two to welcome him into the world. Both were convinced that the baby did not have too great a chance of survival as he was struggling to take his first breath.

Just when they were quite sure he was going to lose the battle, he opened his mouth and let out a loud cry.

Hearing her baby announce his arrival into the world, the woman raised her pale face from under the covers and asked in a soft, feeble voice, "Please, let me see my child before I die."

The surgeon gently placed the little baby in her arms. She gazed at him affectionately, touched his face, and kissed his forehead. Then she fell back in her bed and closed her eyes for one last time.

The surgeon looked at her and declared, "It's all over."

"Poor dear," replied the nurse, carefully picking up the baby.

"Such a good-looking girl," said the surgeon, "I wonder where she came from."

She had been brought there the night before. They had found her lying on the street, her shoes worn out, though where she came from or where she was going was not known to anyone. The surgeon lifted the woman's left hand and commented, "Ah! No ring!" He told the nurse to call him if she had any trouble with the little one, and left.

The nurse began to dress the little baby and wrapped him in an old blanket. The baby cried loudly. Had he known at that moment that he was left an orphan, all alone in the world, to be cared for by the people in the workhouse, he might have cried a little louder.

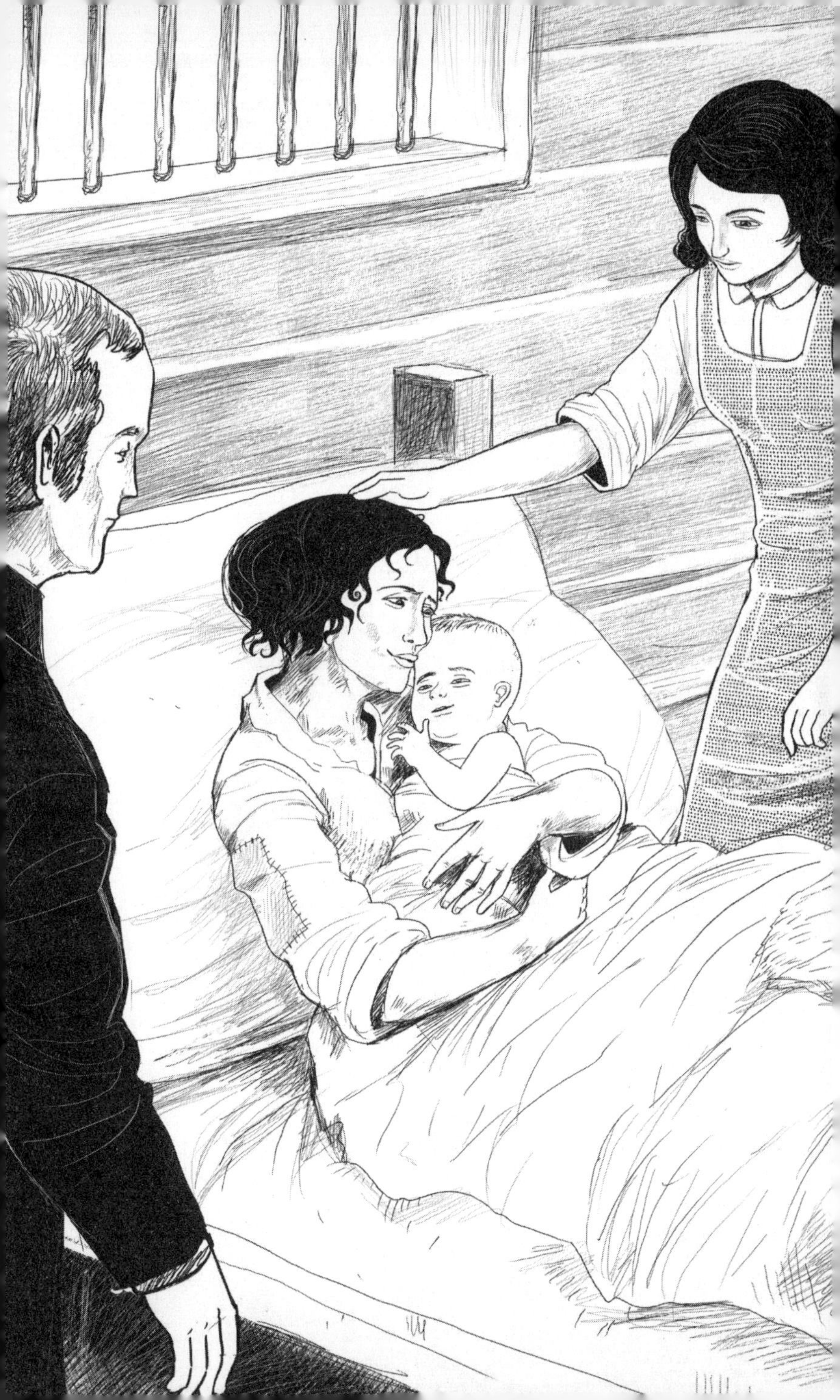

Chapter 2

Early Years

How did Oliver Twist get his name? That job was given to the beadle of the parish, Mr. Bumble. A city official, he was in charge of all the poor and hungry of the parish. Unfortunately, Mr. Bumble was neither kind nor a likable person.

He named the children in alphabetical order; the two before Oliver were S–Swiddle, then came T–Twist. He had names ready right to the end of the alphabet and back. He took Oliver to the workhouse nursery and placed him in the care of Mrs. Mann. She in turn was given a small amount of money to feed, clothe and for the general upkeep of each child. Mrs. Mann however was not an honest woman. She kept most of the money for herself and gave the children very little to eat. Many of the children fell sick from the cold.

On Oliver's ninth birthday, Mr. Bumble paid them a

visit. He often carried a walking cane with him, which he used on any of the children who were being naughty.

When he reached the nursery, Oliver was not there. He had been locked up in a coal shed because he had complained that he was hungry.

He spoke to Mrs. Mann and said, "I have come to take Oliver away, as he is too old to live here. We must put him to work."

Mrs. Mann very quickly wiped the dirt and grime from Oliver's face and hands and took him to meet Mr. Bumble.

"This is Mr. Bumble, Oliver. Now be a good boy and say 'hello'," said Mrs. Mann. "Bow to the gentleman, Oliver," she continued.

Without looking up at Mr. Bumble, but staring at his hat lying on the table, Oliver bowed shyly.

"Oliver! Oliver!" exclaimed Mr. Bumble. "Come here my boy, I haven't seen you for a long time. You have grown into a fine lad!" said he, patting Oliver on the back.

"Oliver, how would you like to come along with me?" asked Mr. Bumble, in a loud voice.

Oliver was about to reply that he would go along with anyone readily rather than live in this place, when he glanced upwards and caught sight of Mrs. Mann. She was standing behind Mr. Bumble's chair, and shaking her fist at him with a threatening look on her face. Oliver had seen this look before. He knew where the fist landed, if anyone did disagree with Mrs. Mann.

He took the hint immediately, and in a sad voice pointed to Mrs. Mann and said, "I'll come with you, if she goes with me."

Mr. Bumble smiled and replied, "Well, she can't come with us right now, can you Mrs. Mann?"

"Not just yet, my boy," said Mrs. Mann.

"But, you don't need to worry. She will definitely come and see you sometimes," said Mr. Bumble.

Tears began to fall from Oliver's eyes as Mrs. Mann gave him a thousand embraces and adjusted the little brown parish cap on his head.

Saying a tearful farewell to Mrs. Mann and holding onto a piece of bread very tightly, he followed Mr. Bumble out of the house. The bread and butter were the first meal he had been given that day. Mrs. Mann had parted with it only because she did not want him to appear too hungry when he reached the workhouse.

Oliver was crying continuously as he said goodbye to the miserable home where he had never heard a single kind word or experienced one kind deed in all his early years.

As the gate closed behind him, he was heartbroken

to leave his little companions behind. After all, they were the only friends he had ever known. A feeling of great sadness and loneliness sank into his little heart for the first time.

As he trotted alongside Mr. Bumble, holding on tightly to his gold-laced cuff, he kept asking him, "Nearly there?"

Within a short while of their arrival at the main workhouse, Oliver was taken by Mr. Bumble into a room where about eight gentlemen sat at a table.

A fat, round faced gentleman, Mr. Limbkins, who was seated at the head of the table asked him what his name was. Oliver was so frightened at the sight of so many men that he began to tremble and started crying.

"You know you're an orphan, I suppose?" said the fat gentleman.

"What's that, sir?" asked Oliver, in a frightened voice.

The gentleman went on to explain to him that an orphan is a person who has no parents.

"Yes," said Oliver simply. Oliver wiped away two or three tears that were rolling down his cheeks.

"What are you crying about?" asked a gentleman in a white waistcoat. He then turned to the others and said, "What could he be crying about?"

"I hope you say your prayers every night, and pray for

the people who feed you, and take care of you," said another gentleman.

"Yes, yes sir," stammered Oliver.

"Well! You don't need to worry," said Mr. Limbkins. "You will be well educated here."

He was then told that he would be taught a useful trade. He would begin work at six in the morning and make string from old pieces of rope.

Mr. Bumble showed Oliver the ward where he was to live. It was a large room with rough, hard beds. Oliver was so upset with the events of the day that he cried himself to sleep.

At the workhouse, the children were all made to work very hard, and they were underfed. Oliver was always hungry. The one person who was happy with the situation at the workhouse was the local coffin maker. The reason for his happiness, however, was the fact that he was always busy taking away the children who could not survive the cruel treatment at the workhouse.

Chapter 3

Please Sir, Some More?

Each day, the meals were had in a large stone hall. The children were given a single bowl of gruel from a large copper pot at one end of the room. It was served by the cook dressed in an apron. What was gruel? It was a very thin, watery soup with a few specks of oatmeal floating in it. On special occasions this was accompanied by a small piece of bread. The moment the gruel was served, the boys hungrily finished every drop of it. The bowls were so clean, they looked like they had been polished, while the boys continued to stare longingly at the pot.

Oliver Twist, along with the other boys, suffered this torture for almost three months; they were now going crazy with hunger.

One of the boys, who was slightly taller than the rest, told the others if he was not given an extra bowl of gruel, he would eat one of them. Frightened, they sat together and came up with a plan. They drew lots. Oliver was chosen for the task. He would have to walk up to the cook and ask for more gruel.

Evening came, and the boys were served their meal which they quickly finished. They nudged Oliver to proceed with the plan. Oliver approached the cook with his empty bowl and spoon in hand.

"Please sir, I want some more."

The room was still with silence. Now, the cook was a fat healthy-looking man. But hearing Oliver he almost fainted. "What?" he cried.

"Please sir, I want some more," repeated Oliver. The cook immediately called for Mr. Bumble, who in turn rushed to the board and informed the man with the round face that Oliver Twist had asked for more.

The punishment was instant. Oliver was locked up in a room without any windows. A notice was posted outside the workhouse offering a reward to anyone who was willing to take Oliver away.

Oliver remained a prisoner in the dark windowless room for almost a week. Occasionally he was allowed to have a wash with icy cold water. He kept crying and hardly slept.

One morning, while Oliver was still confined to his dark and lonely room, Mr. Gamfield, the chimney-

sweep, was passing by the workhouse with his donkey. He was very troubled, as he was unable to pay back certain arrears of his rent which his landlord kept demanding from him.

All of a sudden, he spotted the notice on the workhouse gate. He immediately called out to his donkey to stop. The donkey was pulling a cart laden with two bags of soot. He did not hear his master and continued to jog along.

Running after him, Mr. Gamfield gave the poor animal a whack on his head and, pulling hold of the bridle, turned him round. He then walked up to the gate to read the notice.

The gentleman with the white waistcoat, from the workhouse board, had been standing near the gate and had seen the little quarrel between Mr. Gamfield and his donkey. He was certain that this was exactly the sort of master Oliver Twist needed.

Mr. Gamfield smiled at him. The reward of five pounds was just the amount of money he required.

He spoke to the gentleman, "This boy, sir, I could teach him the right trade. I am a chimney sweep and I am looking for an apprentice. I am willing to take him on," said Mr. Gamfield.

"Come on in," said the gentleman.

Warning his donkey not to run away in his absence, Mr. Gamfield followed the gentleman into the room. It was the same room where Oliver had first been interviewed.

"Isn't chimney sweeping a dangerous trade?" asked Mr. Limbkins, when Mr. Gamfield explained to the gentlemen his plan of taking over the boy.

"Young boys have often been smothered in chimneys," said another gentleman.

"No, no it isn't a bad trade," said Mr. Gamfield. He then went on to explain to the gentlemen the details of the business and why it was not harmful to the boys.

The gentleman in the white waistcoat was amused with his explanations, but Mr. Limbkins was not convinced.

After many more talks the board began to discuss and whisper among themselves.

Finally Mr. Limbkins said, "We have thought about your offer, but unfortunately we do not approve of it."

Mr. Gamfield, twisting his cap in his hands, began walking slowly away from the table.

Pausing near the door, he turned around again and asked, "So is that your final decision? You won't let me have the boy?"

"Yes, we can't. It's a nasty business. But, we might consider giving him to you for less than the initial reward we offered," said Mr. Limbkins.

Mr. Gamfield's face brightened up. Returning to the table, he asked, "What are you willing to give me, gentlemen? Come! Be kind to a poor man. What'll you give me?"

The bargaining continued until they finally decided on an amount of three pounds ten. Mr. Gamfield looked at the faces around the table, and seeing a smile on all of them, gradually began to smile himself.

The bargain was made. Mr. Bumble was informed that Oliver and all his documents had to be taken to the magistrate, who would sign and approve them that very afternoon.

Oliver, to his great astonishment, was freed and ordered to put on a clean shirt. He was given a bowl of gruel by Mr. Bumble. Oliver was so frightened with all this kindness that he began to cry.

"Eat your gruel Oliver, stop crying and be thankful," said Mr. Bumble, "you are going to be made an apprentice."

"An apprentice, what's that?" asked Oliver, still trembling with fear.

"These kind gentlemen on the board, who are like several parents to you, are going to apprentice you and make a man of you. For this, they will be paying a large sum of money. To think they will be spending this money for a naughty orphan whom nobody loves!"

As Mr. Bumble paused to take a breath after making this long speech, tears rolled down Oliver's face, and he sobbed bitterly.

"Come, come Oliver! Wipe away those tears," said Mr. Bumble. "We have to go to the magistrate."

He then informed Oliver about what he had to do.

"Look happy," he said, "and tell the gentleman that you want to be apprenticed."

Oliver promised him that he would obey. He was scared because Mr. Bumble had hinted that if he did not listen, he was not sure what would be done to him.

When they reached the magistrate's office, Oliver was asked to sit in a small room alone. Mr. Bumble said he would come and fetch him when he was required.

Oliver sat waiting for half an hour. Finally, Mr. Bumble arrived and announced in a loud voice, "Oliver, my dear boy, come and meet the gentleman."

In a soft voice he warned, "Remember what I told you."

Oliver was then lead into another large room. Two old gentlemen were seated behind a desk. One was reading the newspaper, while the other was looking at a small piece of parchment paper in front of him.

Mr. Limbkins, Mr. Gamfield and a few other men were also in the room.

Mr. Bumble then said, "Here is the boy, Your Worship."

The old gentleman who was staring at the parchment paper looked up and said, "Oh! So this is the boy."

"Yes sir, this is him," replied Mr. Bumble. Turning to Oliver he said, "Bow to the magistrate, my dear boy."

Oliver obeyed immediately.

"I guess," said the old gentleman, "he's fond of chimney-sweeping, is he?"

"He is very fond of this trade, Your Worship," replied Mr. Bumble. He gave Oliver a gentle pinch, to make sure he did not say otherwise.

"So he wants to be a sweep?" continued the old gentleman.

"If we were to apprentice him to any other trade, I'm sure he would run away, Your Worship," replied Mr. Bumble.

"And his master?" continued the old gentlemen turning to Mr. Gamfield. "Will you treat him well? Will you feed him, and take good care of him?" asked the old gentleman.

"I will, I will," replied Mr. Gamfield.

Looking for his inkstand, the old gentleman suddenly looked straight at Oliver's face and was shocked to see him looking pale and terrified. He was staring at his future master, with horror and fear.

The old gentleman put down his pen, and looked first at Oliver and then at Mr. Limbkins.

Then the old gentleman said to Oliver, "My boy, why are you looking so pale and alarmed? What is troubling you? Don't be afraid, tell me."

Oliver immediately fell down on his knees. Joining his hands, he begged them to take him back to the dark room. They could starve him, beat him, even kill him if they wanted, but he pleaded with them not to send him with this cruel man.

"Well! Of all the cunning orphans I have ever seen, you, Oliver, are the worst," shouted Mr. Bumble.

"Hold your tongue, Mr. Bumble," shouted back the old gentleman.

Turning to Mr. Limbkins, he said, "We will not sign these papers. Now take this child back to the workhouse, and treat him kindly."

The next morning, the notice about the reward for Oliver was back on the gate.

Chapter 4

Life with Mr. Sowerberry

It so happened that there was a death at the workhouse, and the local undertaker, Mr. Sowerberry, was called for. As he was entering the workhouse, he spotted the notice and decided to read what it said. He asked if he could hire Oliver, as he needed a boy to help him with his work. Mr. Bumble agreed, and Oliver was sold off to the undertaker.

Mr. Bumble escorted him to the home of the undertaker and left him there. But not without issuing him a stern warning first, "If you do come back, you will be sent out to sea and drowned."

Mr. Sowerberry introduced young Oliver to his wife, who found him rather small for his age. Mr. Sowerberry convinced her that he would grow, but she was certain that if he did grow, it would only be because they were feeding him well. She kept referring to him as a "bag of bones".

Once Mr. Bumble had left, she pushed him down the stairs into a cold damp room. He was given some of their dog Trip's leftover food. But Oliver was so tired and hungry that he relished the meal. Mrs. Sowerberry was shocked at his appetite.

Holding a dim, dirty lamp in her hand, she then asked Oliver to follow her to the coffin shop. "You don't mind sleeping amongst the coffins, do you?" she asked. Not that poor Oliver had a choice, because there was no other place for him to sleep either way.

Oliver had a very restless sleep that night. He kept expecting to see a body rise up from the unfinished coffins lying around. In fact, he was so frightened, hungry and alone that he kept hoping that his little bed would become his own coffin. He would sleep in it peacefully, in the churchyard compound, with nothing but the sound of the church bell to comfort him.

He was awoken the next morning with the sound of loud kicking outside the shop door. An angry voice yelled at him and said, "I'm Noah Claypole, and you will be working under me."

Oliver drew back the bolts and quickly opened the door, only to be greeted with a kick from the coward Claypole, a charity-boy. One look at Oliver's size, and he was happy to see someone he could kick around.

Oliver followed Noah to the kitchen. Charlotte, a kind maid, had saved a bit of meat for Noah from the master's breakfast. Oliver's meal was just a piece of dried bread.

Weeks passed and Mr. Sowerberry got an idea. He had been observing Oliver who, although good looking, had a sad expression on his face which could be quite appealing. He discussed his plan with his wife. If Oliver was dressed in black, he could lead the procession of mourners at the funerals of children.

His wife found this a brilliant idea. The number of funerals of children was on the rise, and with it, the demand for coffins. The plan worked. Mothers already grieving at the loss of a loved child were touched to see the melancholic Oliver leading the procession.

Oliver was a quick learner and had soon mastered the funeral business. Noah however was extremely jealous of Oliver's success. He kept asking him about his mother and taunting him about his parents.

"She's dead," said Oliver, "of a broken heart", and he pleaded of Noah not to speak about her.

But Noah continued tormenting him, saying she was a bad person and it was better that she was dead, because she would have landed up in prison or been hung.

Oliver was usually a quiet, well-mannered boy, but this statement was too much. He flew into a rage, grabbed Noah by the throat and threw him to the ground.

"He'll murder me. Help! Help!" yelled Noah.

Charlotte and Mrs. Sowerberry rushed in to rescue Noah. They screamed at poor Oliver, punched, beat and scratched him, and finally, dragged him down to the cellar and locked him in.

Mr. Sowerberry was not at home during all this activity. Still not satisfied, and certain that Oliver would just break down the door and free himself at any moment, they asked Noah to run to Mr. Bumble and inform him about what had happened and request him to come over as quickly as he could.

Noah ran as fast as he could to the workhouse, and informed Mr. Bumble that Oliver had tried to murder the three of them.

He returned with a rather angry Mr. Bumble who tried to speak to Oliver, who in turn was in no mood to listen to any of them. He kept kicking at the door and shouting, "Let me out, let me out!"

Mr. Sowerberry finally returned and took over the situation. He dragged Oliver out of the cellar and demanded

to know what had happened. Oliver tried to explain that Noah had said mean things about his mother, but Mrs. Sowerberry agreed with Noah's story. Oliver called her a liar. She was so outraged she began to cry. Mr. Sowerberry beat Oliver and sent him off to bed.

Finally, in the silence of the workshop, Oliver gave way to his feelings. He cried and cried for a long time and finally decided he would run away.

Chapter 5

Oliver Meets Dick

Early the next morning, Oliver tied up some of his clothes into a little bundle, opened the door of the workhouse and ran out into the street.

Running past the village, he suddenly found himself in front of the workhouse nursery. He decided to stop there for a while. Looking into the garden, he saw a boy at work. He was delighted to see that it was his dear friend Dick. Although younger than Oliver, he had been his friend and playmate. Both the boys had spent a lot of time together and had even been beaten and locked up together several times.

He told Dick that he was running away, to seek his fortune, and he shouldn't tell anyone that he had seen him.

Dick climbed up the low gate to give Oliver a hug.

"I hope we meet again," said the frail boy to Oliver. "God bless you."

Even though this blessing came from a young boy, it was the first time Oliver had experienced any form of kindness. Looking back and waving to the boy, Oliver knew he would never forget him.

Chapter 6

The Artful Dodger

Oliver was soon back on the road. He ran, hid behind bushes and continued on his journey, till he was well away from the town and his life with the undertaker.

He finally sat down on the side of the road, all the while wondering what he should do next. He looked at the milestone, it read, "London, 70 miles".

"Ah! London! Surely Mr. Bumble would never find me there," thought Oliver. Besides, he had often heard that you could find work in London.

So tired, but with great determination, Oliver once again set off towards the great city of London.

After being on the road for almost seven days, begging for food and water, sleeping out in the cold in fields and waking up stiff and hungry, his feet sore and legs weak, he finally reached a small town called Barnet, a few miles away from London.

He was resting on a doorstep, wondering what to do next, when he observed an odd-looking boy staring at him. The boy was very short and dirty, with a flat nose and big ears.

"Hello, my friend, what are you doing here?" asked the boy dressed in a man's coat that almost touched his feet. The sleeves of the coat were very long too, and they were rolled back so that his hands were free.

He was almost the same age as Oliver, though he seemed much older.

"I am very hungry and tired," said Oliver. "Been walking for seven days."

"You need some food, and you shall get it," said the boy. So saying, he helped Oliver to his feet and took him to a shop where he bought him some bread and ham. After they had eaten hungrily, he asked Oliver if he was going to London. "Yes!" Oliver replied.

"What about a place to sleep?" asked the boy.

"I don't have one," replied Oliver, "neither do I have any money."

"Well," said the boy, "you don't need to worry. I know an old gentleman who will provide you with a place to stay for nothing, only because you are a friend of mine!"

The boy finally introduced himself to Oliver. "I am Jack Dawkins, but to my friends I'm simply the Artful Dodger."

Chapter 7

Oliver is Welcomed into Fagin's Home

Although his new-found friend seemed strange, Oliver was very happy to accept the invitation. The old gentleman lived in London, and the Artful Dodger was on his way there.

Late at night, after going through a maze of narrow, dirty streets, they arrived at a house. The Dodger held Oliver's arm while they entered a narrow passage. He whistled, and a voice cried out, "Who's there?"

Dawkins was quick to reply, "Plummy and Slam." Oliver was sure this was some kind of signal, for the two of them were led up a flight of broken stairs into a dark room.

The walls and ceiling were black and dirty. An old man was standing near a stove. His hair was long, red and matted. He was busy cooking some sausages.

The Dodger introduced the old man, Fagin, to his new friend Oliver Twist. Huddled around a table were four or five boys in tattered clothes. None of them looked older than the Dodger. They were drinking, smoking long clay pipes and acting much older than their age.

Fagin bowed, and took Oliver's hand saying, "We are very glad to see you, Oliver." Many of the boys got up from their seats and gathered around Oliver. Fagin turned to the Dodger and told him to get the sausages and give Oliver a plate and a place to sit near the fire.

Oliver kept staring around the room. All of a sudden, he spotted a clothesline with a large number of silk handkerchiefs hanging on it.

"Well," said Fagin, "if you are wondering about the handkerchiefs, we have just taken them out to wash. Nothing more to it!"

There was much laughter at this and then they all sat down to supper. Oliver was given some spirit to drink. Before he knew it, he was fast asleep.

Late the next morning, Oliver awoke from a long sleep. The room seemed empty except for old Fagin and himself. Fagin whistled softly as he kept stirring some coffee in a saucepan. Every now and then he would look around and then continue stirring.

Convinced that Oliver was still fast asleep, he locked the door and took out a box from a trap in the floorboard.

Lifting the lid, he took out a magnificent gold watch with sparkling jewels. He kept reaching into the box and pulling out some more watches, brooches, bracelets and other expensive pieces of jewellery.

All of a sudden Fagin looked up and was shocked to see Oliver awake and staring at him. He slammed the box shut with a bang and rushed towards Oliver, with a long bread knife in his hand.

"Are you awake? What have you seen? Speak up for your life!" yelled an almost hysterical Fagin.

"I—I couldn't sleep any longer," stuttered poor Oliver.

"Answer me, what did you see, did you see any of my pretty things?" Fagin demanded.

"Yes, yes," said Oliver. All of a sudden Fagin realized that the boy was being truthful, and he seemed to calm down. His tone changed. He smiled at Oliver and said, "Don't be afraid, they're all mine, my property, I'm a miser and I've stored it all for my old age."

Still scared, Oliver asked if he could get up. Fagin said he could and informed him that there was a jug of water on the table. Oliver walked towards it, and the moment he turned his head the box disappeared.

Shortly, the Dodger and the other boys returned. Charley Bates, a new friend, was with them. They all sat down to breakfast; coffee, hot rolls and ham.

After breakfast, Fagin asked the boys if they had been working hard.

"As hard as nails!" was the reply.

"And what have you got me?" asked Fagin eagerly.

The boys proudly displayed pocket-books, wallets and some handkerchiefs.

Once the breakfast was cleared up, Fagin and the boys began to play a strange game.

Fagin placed a small snuff-box in one of his trouser pockets and a note case in the other. He put a watch in his waist coat pocket with the guard chain round his neck. He stuck a mock diamond pin in his shirt and buttoned up his coat tightly. Having put his spectacle case and handkerchief in his pocket, and holding a stick, he began to pretend that he was walking along the street staring into shop windows. He would stop, look around and pat his pockets, making sure he hadn't lost anything. Oliver found all this very amusing and couldn't stop laughing.

All this time the two boys followed Fagin closely. The moment he stopped, they quickly got out of sight. All of a sudden, the Dodger accidentally trod on his toes and bumped into him. Charley Bates, with great speed, stole his belongings from his pockets. If at any time Fagin felt a hand in his pockets, he would yell, and the game would begin again.

After they had completed several rounds of this rather entertaining game, they had two visitors. Two young women—one named Nancy and the other Bet. Both were rather untidy, with long hair. They were not very pretty but they had much life in their faces. It was only later that Oliver discovered that the two women, along with the boys, were pupils of Fagin.

Once the other young people had gone, Oliver was left alone with Fagin. He was soon involved in the game too.

"Where's my handkerchief? Can you see it hanging out of my pocket?" asked Fagin, walking slowly in front of Oliver.

"Yes, I can, sir," replied Oliver.

"See if you can remove it without me knowing, like you saw your friends doing," said Fagin.

Holding up the pocket with one hand, as he had watched the Dodger doing, Oliver very gently removed the handkerchief from Fagin's pocket with his other hand.

"Have you managed?" asked Fagin, who hadn't felt a thing.

"Here it is!" Oliver exclaimed proudly.

"You are a sharp boy, I'm proud of you," said Fagin.

He was amazed at how quickly Oliver had learnt the skill. He patted him on the head, kept praising him and calling him a clever boy, and even presented Oliver with a silver coin.

Fagin told him that the youngsters had all gone out to work, and if Oliver listened to the boys and copied the way they worked, he too would be a great man someday.

Oliver couldn't understand how stealing and picking someone's pocket could make him great. But he just smiled and agreed with Fagin.

For many days Oliver stayed with Fagin, till finally he got permission to go out to work with the Dodger and Charley Bates. Oliver was excited as he walked between the two boys through the city. He kept wondering what they would do. When they reached a corner, they suddenly stopped. They had seen an old gentleman at a bookstall.

"Do you see that man?" asked the Dodger.

"The man at the bookstall, right?" asked Oliver, excited to be a part of this great adventure.

"Yes, he is just what we require," said Charley.

Within minutes the two boys had walked stealthily towards him. The man had just picked up a book to read and was so engrossed in the book that he was unaware of

his surroundings or the two boys close behind him. The Dodger quietly slid his hand into the man's pocket and stole his expensive silk handkerchief. Oliver watched in horror as the boys ran away. He now understood the mystery behind Fagin's game. The watches, jewellery, expensive handkerchiefs all made sense.

Oliver was so scared that he began to run. At that very instant the gentleman reached for his handkerchief, and finding it missing, turned around sharply only to see Oliver rushing away. Assuming it was Oliver who had stolen his handkerchief, he began to chase after him shouting in a loud voice, "Thief! Thief! Stop him! Stop him!"

Seeing Oliver escaping, a large number of people—the butcher, the baker, and many others—joined the chase. The Dodger and Charley, hiding in a doorway close by, watched, and soon joined in the commotion. They too added to the cries of the crowd, "Thief! Thief!"

All of a sudden, a sharp blow knocked Oliver to the ground. His face was covered with mud and dirt. Within minutes the crowd had gathered around him.

The old gentleman had now reached the spot, and someone asked him if this was the boy.

"Yes! It is," replied the gentleman. "Poor fellow, he seems to have hurt himself," the old gentleman said kindly.

In the meantime, a police officer arrived. He held the half fainting Oliver by the scruff of his neck and pulled him to his feet. He began to drag Oliver towards the police station. The old man walked beside them, all the while wondering where he had seen Oliver before.

Oliver kept whimpering, "But it wasn't me, it wasn't me, it was two other boys," but no one seemed to listen to him. The two real culprits, Charley and the Dodger, watched all the activity and slowly disappeared into the crowd.

Once they had reached the police station, an official began questioning them. He wanted to know who Oliver was and what crime he had committed. The policeman explained that he was a pickpocket and that the man who had been robbed was the old gentleman.

The old gentleman tried to tell the policemen that he was not too sure whether it was Oliver who had robbed him. He did not want to continue with the case.

Each time he looked at Oliver he kept thinking to himself, "There's something about the boy's face, he looks like…" but he simply could not remember. The official, however, insisted that the case be put before a magistrate.

The gentleman was sad and troubled to see Oliver being taken away and locked up in a dirty stone cell. He sat outside and kept reading his book.

After a short time, Oliver was brought to the magistrate's court and made to stand before the magistrate, a rather stern looking man. The policeman explained the case to the magistrate.

The magistrate asked the old gentleman, "Who are you?"

"My name, sir," replied the gentleman, "is Brownlow. I was robbed at a bookstall. I looked around, and seeing the boy fleeing, I shouted and followed him, thinking he was the thief. But to tell you the truth, now I am not very sure if this is the boy who stole my handkerchief, and so I do not wish to press this case any further."

Oliver was standing in one corner and trembling, listening to the conversation between the magistrate and the gentleman.

The magistrate then turned to Oliver and said, "Young rascal, what is your name?"

Oliver was so frightened that he couldn't utter a single word. The clerk moved towards Oliver and tried to get him to reply to the magistrate's question, but he was still unable to say a word. The clerk then took it upon himself to inform the magistrate that Oliver had said his name was Tom White.

The magistrate had his next question ready, "Who and where are your parents?"

The clerk seemed to know all the answers. "He says he has no parents, they died before he was born."

Looking at Oliver, the old gentleman again told the magistrate that he was certain that the boy was unwell and would faint at any moment. He looked pale and weak.

But the magistrate shouted out, "Don't you try to make a fool of me. Let the boy faint if he has to."

As if in response to the magistrate's statement, Oliver fainted and fell heavily to the floor.

The cruel magistrate did not even seem to notice. He kept pounding his hand on the bench and shouted, "I sentence him to three months of hard labor. And now you can all leave my office."

A couple of men came forward to carry Oliver back to his cell. At that moment, there was a commotion as an old man came rushing into the magistrate's office. He shouted, "Stop, stop, don't put him away. He is not the thief."

The magistrate was now really angry. "Throw this man out, and all of you get out of my courtroom!" he yelled.

But the old man kept insisting that he had seen the entire incident. He was the owner of the bookstall.

"And what have you to say?" asked the magistrate, now convinced that this case was not going to end so easily.

"I saw two other boys loitering around, while Mr. Brownlow was reading his book. They were the ones who stole the man's handkerchief. This boy certainly did not commit the robbery. In fact, he was shocked to see it all happen."

"And why did you not come along earlier?" asked the irritated magistrate.

"I didn't have anyone to mind my stall," replied the owner.

"You said," continued the magistrate, "that the gentleman was reading a book?"

"Yes, he was, he still has the book in his hand," replied the man pointing to the book Mr. Brownlow was holding.

"Has he paid for it?" asked the magistrate

"Well, he hasn't," replied the man with a smile.

"Oh! I'm so sorry," said Mr. Brownlow.

"You are really lucky that the bookseller isn't charging you for robbery," said the magistrate.

The magistrate was now left with no choice but to discharge Oliver, who was then carried out onto the street by the men and put down on the pavement. He still looked pale and faint.

The kind-hearted Mr. Brownlow now felt that he was totally responsible for the boy's plight. He therefore decided to take him to his own home and care for him. He called for a coach.

When the coach arrived, he put Oliver in it and he got in from the other side and sat beside him.

"Can I come along with you?" asked the bookstall owner.

"Yes, you can," said Mr. Brownlow. Away they drove towards Mr. Brownlow's home. The coach traveled along a road similar to the one Oliver had taken when he first came to London with the Dodger.

After a while, it finally reached its destination and stopped in front of a neat little house in a quiet street. It was the home of Mr. Brownlow in Pentonville.

Chapter 8

Oliver Finds a Happy Home

Oliver was lifted out of the coach very gently, and taken straight to bed.

He lay in bed for several days with a high fever, most of the time unconscious of what was happening around him. It seemed to him that he was continuously drifting in and out of a very troubled sleep. Finally, weak, pale and extremely tired, he woke up one morning from the fever that had taken a complete hold of him.

A motherly old lady by the name of Mrs. Bedwin was seated at his bedside in an armchair. She was Mr. Brownlow's housekeeper, who had nursed him constantly through his illness. All this while, the doctor too had visited him regularly.

"What has happened to me? Where am I?" asked a confused Oliver.

"You have been very sick, my boy, but now you needn't

worry, you are in safe hands. All is well!" replied Mrs. Bedwin. "Now lie down and rest." She patted his head gently and looked at his face smiling all the while. It was the first time in his life Oliver had ever experienced any kindness from a stranger.

Under her loving care, Oliver soon began to feel better. She was so very kind and gentle with him that Oliver almost felt like he was in heaven.

Within a couple of days, he could get up and sit in the armchair.

Once he was well enough to eat, she brought him a delicious bowl of soup. In Oliver's mind the amount of soup was sufficient to feed around 350 starving orphans at the orphanage. She informed him that Mr. Brownlow would be coming to see him soon and he had to be strong.

As he enjoyed his meal he kept staring at a painting on the wall. He finally turned to Mrs. Bedwin and asked her, "Who is that beautiful young woman in the painting?

"I really don't know," was her reply.

"She is so pretty," continued Oliver, "yet her eyes look so sorrowful. Somehow, wherever I am in the room, her eyes seem to follow me. It's almost as if she is alive and wants to speak to me."

"You are unwell, my child, and you certainly shouldn't

be having such thoughts," said Mrs. Bedwin, worried. "Now back to your soup."

He had almost finished his soup when there was a knock on the door and in walked Mr. Brownlow.

"How are you? Have you had anything to eat?" asked Mr. Brownlow, happy to see the boy, but unhappy to see how pallid and weak he looked.

"I am very well, thank you, sir. I am extremely grateful to you for all the love, kindness and care I am receiving in your home," said Oliver.

"He has just had a bowl of nutritious soup," said Mrs. Bedwin.

"Soup? Ugh! He certainly could do with something better, don't you think so, Tom White?" asked Mr. Brownlow.

"I'm Oliver Twist, sir," replied Oliver.

"That's a strange name, but I remember you telling the magistrate you are Tom White?" said Mr. Brownlow.

"I'm sorry sir, but I didn't," said poor Oliver, worried that the kind gentleman might think he was lying.

"I'm sure it was all a mistake," said Mr. Brownlow, convinced the boy was speaking the truth.

All the while, he kept gazing from the painting of the woman on the wall to Oliver's face. To his astonishment, the resemblance was unbelievable. He felt Oliver was a living copy of the woman. The eyes, the mouth, the head, every feature seemed the same. He pointed this out to Mrs. Bedwin.

Chapter 9

Where is My Boy?

Now that they had lost Oliver, Charley Bates and the Dodger feared their meeting with Fagin. As expected, Fagin was mad with rage when he found they had lost his most promising student.

He grabbed the Dodger by the neck shouting, "You young hounds, where's Oliver? Speak up or I'll throttle you!"

"The police have got him, please, please let me go," begged a frightened Dodger. Now Fagin's greater fear was what Oliver would say to the police. In his anger he picked up a pot and flung it at the Dodger. The Dodger ducked, the pot missed him, and almost hit a strongly built man who had just walked in through the doorway. It was Bill Sikes, a man of about 35 years of age.

"What's all the commotion? What's going on, Fagin? Are you ill-treating my boys?" growled Bill, in a hoarse voice.

Bill had a black eye and a scruffy beard. He had on a brown hat and a dirty handkerchief was wrapped around his neck. He wore a long black coat with dirty trousers. He was followed by a thin, beaten up bull terrier called Bull's-eye. The dog sneaked into the room and quietly sat in a corner.

Bill Sikes, a humorless man, was Fagin's partner in crime.

"Not so loud, not so loud, Mr. Sikes, you might give us away," said Fagin, trembling.

"Don't call me mister, don't you know my name?" Bill asked angrily.

"I certainly do Bill, and I also notice that you are in an unpleasant mood today."

Bill asked the two boys to tell him their story. He now understood that this young boy, Oliver, who knew their business secrets, was in the custody of the police. Somehow or the other they had to get him back before he said something that would get them all into trouble.

"Well," said Bill, "this is serious; you'll certainly be behind bars, Fagin."

"If the game's up, it will be worse for you more than me," Fagin grumbled.

There was silence for a couple of moments till Sikes

suddenly said, "There's no way out, we have to find out what happened to the boy. If he hasn't squealed about us and is locked in jail, that's fine. We will have to wait till he is out, and then decide the next step. But we must find him first!"

The problem was, none of them wanted to go, or be seen, anywhere near the police station or the courthouse.

As luck would have it, as they spoke, Nancy, Bill Sikes' girlfriend, walked in.

"Just the person we need!" cried Fagin. "You'll help us out and go, won't you?"

"Go where? And why?" asked a confused Nancy, trying to sort out what was happening.

"To the courthouse," said Fagin.

"No, I shan't," said Nancy.

"You have to! Bill, she has to. You must convince her," said Fagin in a rather upset and excited voice.

"She will go Fagin, I assure you," said Bill.

Finally, after a lot of discussion, it was agreed that Nancy would go to the courthouse. She would go in a straw hat, holding a basket, and wearing a proper dress, looking for her dear little brother Oliver who was lost. "This will make her look very respectable," Fagin thought shrewdly.

Nancy, looking very presentable, made her way towards the courthouse. Going through the back gates, she reached the cells and gently tapped on the door.

"Oliver, Oliver?" she called in a soft voice. She could hear no sound.

Nancy suddenly observed a tramp in one of the cells.

"Have you seen a little boy here?" Nancy asked.

The tramp said he hadn't.

Nancy walked on in search of the clerk. She would request him to set her brother free.

"Well," said the clerk, "if I don't have him, how can I set him free?"

"Then where is my brother?" cried Nancy, pretending to be really upset.

"He's with the gentleman," replied the clerk.

"Gentleman? Which gentleman has taken away my poor brother?" asked Nancy.

The clerk then explained to Nancy how the owner of the bookstall had informed the magistrate that Oliver was innocent. Mr. Brownlow, the old gentleman, had taken him home with him to care for him as he was very unwell.

Nancy ran back to Fagin's home to give them the news. Fagin was desperate.

"We must get him back!" he shouted.

He chased all the boys away as he did not want anyone around. Locking the door behind him, he quickly took out

his precious box and hid all the watches, jewelry and other objects in his pockets.

He thought to himself, "Although he hasn't betrayed us yet, he could do it very soon. We must set up a plan to capture him from Mr. Brownlow's home."

Chapter 10

Oliver Visits the Bookshop

Oliver spent the happiest days of his life at Mr. Brownlow's.

One day he noticed the painting on the wall had disappeared. When he asked what had happened to it, Mrs. Bedwin explained that Mr. Brownlow felt it would upset him and prevent his speedy recovery and so had asked for it to be removed. Oliver tried to explain to Mrs. Bedwin that he really liked the painting, but nothing was said about the painting again.

With all the love and care, Oliver was recovering fast. He was so happy in his new home; everything was peaceful and quiet, and everyone treated him gently and kindly. He had spoken to Mr. Brownlow and told him his sad life story.

Mr. Brownlow got him a new suit, a cap and shoes. Oliver was delighted. He gave away his old clothes to one of the maids who had been kind to him.

One day, Mr. Brownlow sent for him. Mrs. Bedwin quickly got him ready to go to Mr. Brownlow's study. As she saw him leave, she was happy at the way he looked. He had grown into a handsome young boy.

Oliver however was a bit worried, because he thought Mr. Brownlow had called for him only to ask him to leave.

When he entered the study, he found Mr. Brownlow reading a book. The old man spoke kindly to Oliver, but Oliver was frightened. He begged him not to send him away. He would work as his servant, do anything, but he did not want to be thrown out onto the streets again.

Mr. Brownlow assured him that he would never do that, he would always be his faithful friend, unless of course Oliver cheated on him.

While they spoke, there was a knock on the door. The visitor was a friend of Mr. Brownlow, Mr. Grimwig. He was an old, stern looking gentleman. Mr. Grimwig wanted to know who the boy was. Mr. Brownlow promptly introduced him as the young Oliver Twist. Mr. Grimwig kept looking at Oliver and you could tell that he did not trust him one bit. Mr. Brownlow, however, said that he could trust him with his life.

"We shall see, time will tell," said Mr. Grimwig with an unhappy look on his face.

At that moment, there was another knock on the door. It was Mrs. Bedwin holding some books in her hand. "Ask the boy who delivered these books from the bookstall to wait, I need to return some books to him," said Mr. Brownlow.

Mrs. Bedwin rushed to look for the boy, but he had left. "Why don't you ask Oliver to return them for you?" suggested Mr. Grimwig.

Oliver in turn was very happy to run an errand for Mr. Brownlow. "I'll take them, sir," he replied.

"Thank you, Oliver. Here, take this money with you. I owe it to the bookseller. Bring back the ten shillings change." So saying, he handed five pounds to Oliver.

"I won't take more than ten minutes sir," Oliver said, excited. He then bowed to Mrs. Bedwin and left.

"Do you think he will actually come back?" asked Mr. Grimwig the moment Oliver had stepped out. "Of course he will, why won't he?" replied Mr. Brownlow.

"Well," said Mr. Grimwig, "you have clad him well, bought him a new suit, and given him money too. He has all the reason to go back to his old lifestyle and his old friends. I can guarantee, you will never see him again."

As Oliver walked along towards the bookstall, thinking how blessed he was, he was startled by a young woman who

cried out in a loud voice, "Oh my dearest brother, I've finally found you!"

With these words she grabbed him and threw her arms around his neck. The woman was Nancy, whom Oliver did not recognize.

"Who are you? Don't stop me, let me go," cried an astonished Oliver.

"It's me, your sister! How cruel of you to run away! You must come home with me, right this moment," exclaimed the woman, breaking into loud sobs.

She then turned around and began to inform all the passersby that this naughty brother of hers had run away from his family a month ago. He had broken his mother's heart and preferred to stay with his new friends who were a pack of thieves.

Oliver was shocked to hear all this and kept saying that it was not true; he was an orphan with no family.

Looking closely at the woman's face he suddenly recognized her.

"Why," he said, "it's Nancy!"

"Do you see?" cried Nancy. "He recognizes me!"

At that moment, Bill Sikes suddenly came forward with his dog and said, "Oliver, how could you do this to your mother? Come home immediately."

"Please, please help me, I don't know these horrible people," shouted Oliver.

"What are you doing with these books, you rascal? Have you stolen them?" Bill grabbed Oliver. Oliver tried to free himself from Sikes' clutches, but he was weak, overpowered and helpless. He struggled but he could do nothing more.

Bill struck him hard and dragged him through the streets of London. Oliver went along with them, his cries now only whimpers.

Chapter 11

A Reward of Five Pounds

It was dark and the gas lights were lit. Mrs. Bedwin would not leave the door. She stood anxiously, waiting for Oliver to return. She had sent the servant several times up and down the street, but there was no sign of Oliver.

In the meantime, even as it grew dark, Mr. Grimwig and Mr. Brownlow kept sitting in the parlor, with the watch between them. Mr. Brownlow was hoping and praying that his dear Oliver would return.

Some days later, while Mr. Bumble was going through the newspaper, he was surprised to see an advertisement in the first paragraph he saw.

A reward of five pounds was being offered to anyone who had information about a young boy by the name of Oliver Twist. He had run away or had possibly been taken away against his will from his home in Pentonville. Anyone who had any knowledge about his previous history could also claim the reward.

The advertisement contained a complete description of the outfit Oliver was wearing and his appearance along with the name and address of Mr. Brownlow. After having read and reread the advertisement several times, Mr. Bumble was soon on his way to visit Mr. Brownlow.

Mr. Bumble was greeted by a young girl who opened the door and asked what his business with her master was. Hearing the name Oliver, Mrs. Bedwin rushed to the door and welcomed him in. Mr. Bumble was soon shown into the study where Mr. Brownlow was seated, as usual, with his friend Mr. Grimwig.

"Where is Oliver? How do you know him? What do you know about him?" Mr. Brownlow asked worriedly.

"Nothing good for sure," added Mr Grimwig.

Mr. Bumble put down his hat, nodded his head, and began his story. "Oliver was an orphan but had always been an ungrateful child. One night he attacked an innocent boy, for no reason at all, and ran away from his master's house."

Mr. Bumble provided all these details and more. Then shaking his head gravely, he pocketed the five pounds given to him by Mr. Brownlow and left.

Mr. Brownlow was sad and disheartened to hear the

story. He called out to Mrs. Bedwin and said, "It is sad, but true, Oliver has deceived us. I don't want to hear his name mentioned in this house ever again."

Mrs. Bedwin tried to say that this was surely not possible, but Mr. Brownlow had decided. They had been deceived. There was great sadness at Mr. Brownlow's house that evening.

Chapter 12

Oliver is Back

Along the route, Sikes kept tormenting Oliver. With his hand around Oliver's neck, he spoke to his dog, "Listen Bull's-eye! One word from him and you catch him by the throat!" The dog, as if understanding his master and his responsibility perfectly, growled and glared at Oliver.

They were finally back at Fagin's house. Fagin, the Dodger and Charley were delighted to see him again.

"I'm so happy to see you again, my dear Oliver," said Fagin, bowing to him as if he were royalty.

"Take a look at his clothes, Fagin! He has certainly turned into quite a gentleman," Charley chuckled.

"Don't worry, Oliver. The Dodger will provide you with another set of clothes. We don't want you to spoil this new suit, now do we?" grinned Fagin.

In the meantime, the Dodger had already found the money given to him by Mr. Brownlow.

As he pulled it out Sikes exclaimed, “Hey, what’s that?’

He was about to take it from the Dodger when Fagin stepped forward and grabbed the money.

“That’s clearly mine,” shouted Fagin.

“No! It’s mine! It belongs to me and Nancy, and if you don’t return it this very moment, I will take the boy back,” Sikes shouted back.

“Don’t you dare!” yelled Fagin.

“But this is not fair. Give it to me, this moment. What do you think? That Nancy and I have nothing better to do than look for a boy who suddenly disappears and is handed over to the police? Give us the money right now, you lazy old Jew!” With these words he grabbed the money from Fagin.

All the while, Oliver was silently watching the great battle for his money from a corner. He kept looking from Fagin to Sikes and back to Fagin. Realizing that they were occupied with their greed and were not paying any attention to him, he suddenly jumped to his feet and rushed out of the room. It was his last desperate attempt at freedom.

He was instantly followed by Fagin, the Dodger and Charley Bates who tried in vain to stop him from fleeing. His cries for help echoed through the room.

As he attempted to rush through the doorway, he was caught by the burly Sikes. Oliver would have been torn to pieces by Bull's-eye had it not been for Nancy who rushed to his help. She was greatly saddened by the look of fear and grief on his face and wanted to protect him from the violence.

"Hold back that dog," she yelled, "it will kill the boy!"

Sikes in turn shouted at her and told her to get away or he would get rid of her as well.

"I'm not afraid of you," she shouted back. But before she knew it, Sikes had pushed her, and she flew to one end of the room.

Oliver was dragged into the room by Fagin and the boys.

"So, you tried to get away, did you?" cried Fagin. "We'll make sure you never try to escape again."

He then rushed to the fireplace, and picking up a piece of firewood, began to hit Oliver with it.

Nancy could not control herself. She rushed to Fagin, snatched the firewood from him and flung it away.

"I won't allow you to hurt this boy anymore, Fagin! You could kill him with your temper," Nancy cried. "Aren't you satisfied you have him back?"

An argument arose between Nancy and Fagin. Nancy was so upset, she ran at Fagin and was about to hit him, when Sikes got in the way and held her. This was all too much for Nancy; she struggled a bit and then fainted.

"Well she won't be much trouble now," said Sikes putting her down in one corner of the room.

Fagin wiped his forehead and smiled. He was relieved that the trouble was over, although fights and arguments like this were common in his house, and neither he, nor Sikes, nor Bull's-eye, nor the boys, seemed too troubled or disturbed by it.

"It's worse when we have to deal with women," said Fagin, "but they are clever, and we would never be able to continue our business without them."

Fagin then asked Charley to take Oliver to bed in the adjacent kitchen.

"We better take off his best clothes too as he wont be needing them," said Charley.

"He certainly won't be needing them," replied Fagin with a grin.

Charley led Oliver away to the kitchen where there were two beds. He asked him to take off his fancy clothes and gave him a set of old clothes in return. Oliver did as he was told.

"Don't worry about your smart clothes," said Charley, "I'll give them to Fagin, he will take good care of them."

Charley pointed out his bed to him, and left him in the dark room, locking the door behind as he left.

Oliver, now sick and very tired, was soon fast asleep.

Chapter 13

New Plans for Oliver

The next morning, after Charley and the Dodger had left for their day's work, Fagin spoke to Oliver.

"Why are you so ungrateful? Do you know what happens to boys who are ungrateful and speak to the police?" he asked.

Oliver sat silently.

"The last one," continued Fagin, "was caught and hung, even before he could tell his story. Remember, I won't harm you anymore. Just trust me. You are a clever boy and you will understand. We can definitely be friends again."

Having finished the conversation and convinced that Oliver had understood the seriousness of what would happen to him if he disobeyed, he left the room. He locked the door behind him and went out into the cold windy street.

After a short distance he reached a dark alleyway and

knocked on the door.

"Who is it?" called a voice from inside. A dog growled in the background.

"It's me," replied Fagin.

"You may enter," said Sikes.

Fagin was surprised to see Nancy there. He was not sure if Nancy would be happy to see him. They had not met each other since the day of Oliver's return and their argument. Nancy did not say a word.

Fagin walked towards the fireplace and sat down.

"Well Bill, to continue with our plan, are we carrying out the robbery?"

"Not until I get the right person for the job," said Sikes. "I need a boy, a small boy."

"That's just what I came to discuss with you. I have the perfect candidate for you. Oliver! It's time we put him back to work. And besides, the other boys are too big for the job. All you need to do is frighten him a bit, and he'll do simply anything for you," said Fagin.

"And when do you plan to carry out this great project?"asked Nancy.

"Night after tomorrow," replied Sikes.

"The perfect day, there will be no moon," said Fagin, with a smile on his face. He was happy to be going ahead with the plan. The two continued plotting together.

Finally, it was decided that Nancy would visit Fagin's home the next evening to pick up Oliver.

Oliver was surprised when he awoke the next morning to find a new pair of shoes placed at his bedside.

At breakfast, Fagin informed him that he would be going to Bill Sikes' house that night. Oliver, on hearing the name Sikes, looked frightened. But Fagin assured him that he needn't worry, and Sikes would return him to them shortly.

That evening as Fagin was getting ready to go out, he spoke to Oliver.

"Take this candle and this book," he said. "Keep reading till they come to get you."

He also warned Oliver to do as he was told as Bill was a villain. Then he gave Oliver a frightening grin and left.

In a short while, Nancy walked in. She didn't look too well and trembled slightly.

"Where are you taking me?" asked a frightened Oliver.

"Don't worry boy, no harm will come to you."

"I don't trust you," said Oliver.

"If I could help you out of this situation I would, Oliver, but I simply can't. Had someone else come to fetch you, they would have been far worse than me. Just remember one thing. Whatever they ask you to do is not your fault."

So saying, she held his hand and the two hurried off.

A cart was waiting outside for them. The driver lashed his horses and drove them at great speed to Bill Sikes' house.

They were greeted with a loud "Hello!" from Sikes. He held Oliver by the shoulder and made him stand in front of him while he sat at the dining table.

Picking up a pistol that was lying on the table he seriously asked Oliver, "Have you seen something like this before? Do you know what damage it can do?"

"Yes," said a frightened Oliver.

He then held the pistol close to Oliver's temples and said, "One word from you when we are outdoors, except when I speak to you, and you will have a bullet through your head."

Oliver believed every word he said. "Yes, yes sir," he replied, trembling.

Sikes then told Oliver to rest awhile, and they would wake him up when they were ready to leave.

When he was awoken, he watched as Sikes kept putting a variety of things in his pocket.

Sikes held Oliver's hand and together they stepped outside. It was dawn on a quiet cheerless morning. There was a wind blowing, and it was also raining. The streets

were empty when they started their journey, but as they walked along the shops began to open and people started moving around. Sikes kept telling him to "hurry, hurry!" as they hastened along.

They walked on to the other side of the big city. Occasionally, Sikes would ask a cart driver to give them a lift. He would take them a short distance and then they would continue tramping.

Oliver was very tired and frightened. He did not know where Sikes was taking him. They had been walking for hours on end, eating in public houses, then walking on again.

They finally stopped at a solitary, dilapidated house. Sikes, still holding Oliver's hand, went up to the door and opened it.

They were invited in by a rough voice. The room was dark and smoky, and two men were seated inside.

One of the men, Toby Crackit, was smoking a pipe. He was very smartly dressed.

"Hello Sikes! Who have we here?" exclaimed Crackit.

"He's Oliver, the boy I spoke of," said Sikes.

"You mean one of Fagin's boys?" asked Barney, the other man in the room.

Preparations for the "job" began. Pistols, ropes, lamps,

keys, etc. Nothing was forgotten.

Then, holding Oliver's hands, Sikes and Crackit set off again. Barney stayed behind.

They crossed a bridge and were soon in a new town. The church bells struck two. They continued walking for a quarter of a mile till they reached a house that was surrounded by a wall.

Within a second Crackit had climbed over it. Oliver was pushed up next. Before he had time to even think about what was really happening, he was lying with Toby in the grass, on the other side of the wall. He was followed by Sikes. The three began to creep silently along the wall.

For the first time Oliver realized the implication of what was happening; housebreaking, robbery, probably even murder.

He was frightened and begged of them, "Please, please let me go, I don't want to steal!

But Sikes only put a pistol to his head and cursed him. Toby immediately knocked the pistol out of Sikes' hand saying, "Hold it Bill, this is not the time."

Then he looked at Oliver and said, "If I hear one more word from you I myself will crack your head open."

Sikes kept silently cursing Fagin for having sent Oliver

for this job.

Using a crowbar he wrenched the shutter of a little window open. The window was close to the ground at the back of the house and just large enough for Oliver to go through.

Sikes whispered to Oliver, "I am going to let you in through this window. Take this lamp, go up the steps and along the hall to the front door. When you reach it, open it and let us in."

Sikes lifted Oliver onto Crackit's back, and then holding onto his collar, landed him safely, feet-first, on the floor inside. He then handed the lamp over to Oliver and warned him that if he tried any tricks, he was within range of Sikes' pistol. If he did falter, he would shoot him in an instant.

"Okay!" whispered Oliver, terrified. He, however, had decided that whether he survived or not he would warn the family in the house about the robbery. He began to run.

"Come back! Come back!" yelled Sikes. Suddenly there was a flash and a burst of smoke. Two men were seen at the top of the stairs. Oliver staggered backwards only to be grabbed by Sikes and pulled out of the window. Sikes fired back at the two men.

"The boy has been hit, give me your scarf!" he cried.

Soon there was more action; shouts, bells ringing, shots being fired. Knowing they were being pursued, Sikes dropped Oliver, threw a scarf over him, and the two disappeared into the night.

Oliver lay in the bushes. It was raining heavily, but he could not feel it. He was soon unconscious and could see or hear no more.

Chapter 14

The Secret

In the meantime, Mrs. Corney, the matron who was in charge of the workhouse where Oliver was born, had a visitor. It was Mr. Bumble. She offered him some tea which he readily agreed to and seated himself beside her. This made Mrs. Corney's cheeks turn pink, but she continued sipping on her tea.

"Would you like some more sugar, Mr. Bumble?" she asked, holding up the sugar bowl towards him.

"Yes ma'am, thank you," he quickly replied. He continued to stare at her and gently moved his chair towards her. Once he had finished his tea and wiped his lips, he gave her a kiss and put his arm around her.

Mrs. Corney was in such shock that she was about to scream, but she had lost her voice.

At that moment, there was a knock on the door, and an old woman appeared.

"Please, please, come along with me. Old Sally is going fast," she said.

"But how can I be of any help?" asked Mrs. Corney.

"She wants to tell you something, which only you must hear," pleaded the old woman.

Mrs. Corney agreed to go along. She asked Mr. Bumble to wait for her and followed the old woman.

They came to a room where a sick woman was lying in bed. At her side sat another old woman, who seemed to be watching over the invalid. Mrs. Corney gently asked both the old women to leave so that she could be alone with Mrs. Sally Thingummy.

"I need to tell you something in your ears," whispered Mrs. Thingummy. She slowly tried to raise her head from the bed.

"In this very room," continued the sick lady, "I once cared for a frail young woman. She died after giving birth to her son."

"But, what has that to do with both of us?" asked a confused Mrs. Corney.

The sick woman's face turned red. "You don't understand," she said, "I stole from her."

"Stole! What did you steal from her?" cried Mrs. Corney impatiently.

"Gold! The only thing that she possessed," continued the dying woman.

"Gold! What gold? What did you do with it? Where is it?" cried Mrs. Corney, bending right over the dying woman.

"All she asked me to do was to keep it safe. For if they had only known…"

"Who are they? Known what? Tell me quickly," begged Mrs. Corney.

"The boy was a copy of his mother," said the sick woman.

"Do you know the boy's name?" asked Mrs. Corney.

"Oliver," said Mrs. Thingummy weakly. "The gold that I stole was…"

"Tell me—what happened?"

But at that moment the sick woman fell back on her bed, dead.

Mrs. Corney was so distressed that she hurried back home.

Mr. Bumble was still there.

"Why are you so troubled? What has happened?" asked Mr. Bumble.

"Oh dear, I'm very upset, I've just heard some terrible news," she cried.

"Don't worry about it, ma'am," said Mr. Bumble.

Mrs. Corney soon stopped shaking and crying. The two sat together in silence for some time. After a while, Mrs. Corney very slowly put her hand on Mr. Bumble's. He in turn kissed her.

Mr. Bumble then bent over her and said, "The little word? That one little word, Mrs. Corney."

"Yes, I will marry you!" cried Mrs. Corney joyfully.

"And when will the day be?" continued Mr. Bumble.

Mrs. Corney could not suppress her joy any longer. Throwing her arms round Mr. Bumble's neck she said, "As soon as you please, Mr. Bumble."

The marriage contract was solemnly marked with a cup of tea.

As they later sat together and chatted, Mrs. Corney told Mr. Bumble all about Sally's death. Mr. Bumble wanted to know what had upset her.

"Nothing really," said Mrs. Corney.

"But don't you think you need to tell me?" asked Mr. Bumble.

"Not right now, my dear. Once we're married," she replied.

Mr. Bumble could do nothing to persuade her, so he had to be satisfied with her reply.

Chapter 15

Fagin has a Visitor

Mr. Fagin was seated in his house, the same place from where Nancy had picked up Oliver, brooding. The Dodger and Charley Bates were also in the room when the bell rang, and the Dodger went to the door to see who it was. He returned and whispered something in Fagin's ear.

"What do you mean? Alone?" shouted Fagin. The Dodger shook his head.

"Let him in," said Fagin.

A man entered with his face covered by a scarf. He looked around then slowly removed the scarf. It was Toby Crackit.

"Fagin, where is Bill?" asked Crackit.

"What do you mean? How should I know? Where are Sikes and Oliver?" said Fagin angrily.

"I'm guessing you know that the robbery was a failure," said Crackit.

"Yes, I know, what happened that hasn't already been reported?"

So saying Fagin took out a newspaper from his pocket and pointed at it.

"The boy was fired at, and he was hurt. We carried him away, but they chased us. We couldn't protect him any longer, or we all would have been caught. We left him in a ditch. Whether he is still dead or alive, we have no idea," said Crackit.

Fagin left the house immediately. He rushed into the nearest public house, The Three Cripples. He seemed to be looking for someone.

The inside of The Three Cripples was dark and full of smoke. It was impossible to see anyone clearly.

"Can I help you Mr. Fagin?" asked a voice from near the door.

"Yes, you can, I need to see him," said Fagin.

"Are you looking for Monks?" enquired the man again.

"Yes, yes you are right," whispered Fagin impatiently.

"Will you wait for a few minutes; he'll be here…"

"I'm sorry, I can't," said Fagin. "Inform him that I came to visit him, and he should see me tomorrow."

Then he was off again, this time in search of Sikes. When he reached Mr. Sikes' residence, he told Nancy what

Crackit had revealed to him about the robbery and the condition of Oliver. She began to cry, and tears rolled down her cheeks.

When Fagin questioned her about Sikes, she said she really didn't know where he was. As for the boy, Nancy said she was convinced that he would be better off anywhere but with them.

Fagin told her that Oliver was worth a lot of money and had to be found.

Fagin left Nancy and was back on the road. It was now almost midnight. As he turned the corner of his own street, a dark figure suddenly appeared in front of him from the shadows of a doorway.

He suddenly heard a whisper, "Fagin! It's me!"

"You, Monks?" asked Fagin.

"What have you been up to?" inquired Monks.

"Been about your business. Nothing good though," said Fagin.

"Nothing bad, I hope," said Monks looking at Fagin in a startled manner.

They had just arrived at the house. Fagin unlocked the door and asked Monks to close it gently behind him.

He then lit a candle and asked Monks to follow him upstairs.

Both men began to speak to each other in whispers.

"I'm sure it was all planned badly. You shouldn't have sent him on that robbery. All I asked you to do was to turn the boy into a pickpocket so that he was convicted."

"Certainly not," said Fagin. "He could not be trained and would certainly have been caught."

Monks' motives were mysterious. He had seen Oliver only once before in his life, the day Oliver had been arrested. For some reason he hated Oliver. He had some plan for Oliver that was clear to no one but himself.

All of a sudden Monks cried, "Look!"

"Where, what?" asked Fagin.

"I saw the shadow of a woman with a bonnet," said Monks. They both ran out of the room as the candle slowly burned out. But all they saw was an empty staircase.

"All your imagination, Monks, there's no one there," said Fagin.

"I tell you Fagin, I swear, I saw it. It was bending over, when I spoke it disappeared."

They searched in vain in all the rooms, they were all cold and empty. They even went down into the cellars, but everything was quiet, nothing moved.

Chapter 16

At Mrs. Maylie's Home

When Oliver awoke, he found himself lying on the cold ground where Sikes and Crackit had left him. The men who were looking for the thieves had not been able to find him in the darkness. He was weak, felt faint and was covered in blood. This was because of the loss of blood from the shot in his arm. He could hardly move. He tried to stand up, but fell back in pain.

Finally, dizzy and half-conscious, he managed to stagger towards a house. Then he remembered the place. It was the same house they had been trying to rob. He remembered climbing up the wall. He felt like running away, but was too weak to even stand. As he was about to fall unconscious, he knocked faintly on the door and sank onto the steps.

Mr. Giles, the butler, and the other servants were seated around the fire in the kitchen. Mr. Brittles, the cook, and the maid were there too. They were discussing the robbery. Mr. Giles was just narrating to them how he had shot one of the thieves, and he and Mr. Brittles had chased them, when they heard a sound at the door.

Within a minute, Mr. Giles was at the door and looking down at a small boy.

"Isn't this one of the thieves?" asked Mr. Giles. "I'm sure he is the one I shot."

At that moment someone called out from the top of the stairs to Giles.

"Giles, can you please tell me what's happening?" asked the young woman who was Rose Maylie. She was the niece of Mrs. Maylie, the owner of the house.

"He's one of the thieves, miss; I shot him," answered Mr. Giles proudly.

"Don't speak so loudly Mr. Giles, you will wake up my aunt. Is the boy badly hurt?" asked Rose.

"Yes, miss, he is," replied a heartless Mr. Giles. Some of the servants immediately picked up Oliver by one leg and one arm and dragged him into the room. Mr. Brittles held up a light over him.

"I must speak to my aunt," said a worried Rose. She was not happy at the thought of a young wounded thief

lying in her house.

Soon she was back and asked them to carry the boy upstairs to a bedroom. She then asked Mr. Brittles to go and get the doctor immediately. The doctor soon arrived.

For the second time in his life, just when he had given up all hope, Oliver experienced kindness again. He was now in the home of a kind old lady, Mrs. Maylie, and her young adopted niece who was about seventeen years of age. Both ladies were still quite shocked at the attempted burglary and that the wounded thief was lying in their home. Once Dr. Losberne had examined Oliver he asked them to accompany him into the room to see the patient.

"You must see the thief," he insisted. Hesitantly, they followed him up the stairs, into the room. As the curtains were drawn aside, they were shocked to see a small boy instead of a ruffian lying on the bed. He was in pain; his arm was wounded and bandaged across his chest.

"This is definitely not a criminal, it's an innocent child!" cried the old lady. The boy seemed to smile in his sleep as Rose bent gently over him.

The doctor informed them that there was a possibility that the child may have been a tool of the robbers.

"The poor boy, I wonder if he ever knew what it was

like to have a good home. Please Aunt, don't let them take him to prison, you must be merciful to him," begged Rose.

Mrs. Maylie asked the doctor how she could save him. He informed her that the best way was to convince Giles that he had shot the boy by mistake.

"The boy should wake up in an hour or so," said the doctor. "We can then speak to him about his past life, and if we find that he is a criminal, we will hand him over to the police."

"If he's not, then he can stay with us," said Rose.

It was only in the evening that they were able to question Oliver. In a soft tired voice, he told them his story. He told them about all the evil men he had met and all the hardships they had brought to him. Everyone who listened was moved by his sad experiences and convinced that he was not a criminal. He fell back into a peaceful sleep.

The doctor then went down to speak to the servants. They were all sitting together discussing the events of the previous night.

"How is our patient tonight?" asked Mr. Giles.

"I'm afraid you have got yourself into some trouble, Giles," replied the doctor.

"Is he going to die sir?" asked a frightened Giles.

"Well, that is not the point," said the doctor. "Tell me, are you and Brittles willing to swear that the young boy lying wounded upstairs is the same one that came through the window late last night?"

The doctor, who was usually calm, was now quite angry. Both Mr. Giles and Mr. Brittles sensed his mood and were confused.

"Someone has broken into the house, and in the darkness, two men see a boy in between the smoke," continued the doctor. The next thing we see is a boy, wounded in the arm, bleeding, and these two men swear that he is the thief. Now the question is, were these men justified in saying this?"

Both the accused now looked doubtfully at each other.

The discussion in the kitchen was interrupted by a knock at the door. The door was opened for two police officers, and they were led upstairs to Oliver's room by the doctor.

The doctor pointed out Oliver to the policemen. He explained that the boy had come for help and had been treated violently by the gentlemen because they thought he was a thief. When questioned by the policeman, all Giles could say was that he thought the boy was the thief from the night before. After much questioning he was finally convinced Oliver wasn't the thief.

The police officer concluded that the two gentlemen had made a mistake.

As for Mrs. Maylie and Rose, they had both taken a liking to Oliver and were determined to protect the poor orphan. Rose herself was an orphan who had been saved from eternal loneliness by Mrs. Maylie.

The police officer agreed to allow Oliver to stay with Mrs. Maylie and Rose.

Oliver made a slow recovery at Mrs. Maylie's. The two kind ladies kept showering love and tender care on him. He began to feel better. He often spoke to them about how grateful he was and how he wished to repay their kindness by serving them always.

"I have been an ungrateful boy once," he told Rose.

"What do you mean?" Rose wanted to know.

"Mr. Brownlow, the kind gentleman who cared for me before, doesn't even know what happened to me," explained Oliver.

"He certainly would want to know that you are well," replied Rose.

"I just wish I can see him again someday, and tell him

the true story," sighed Oliver.

"Yes, you must. Dr. Losberne will drive you there in the coach, once you have regained your strength," said Rose.

A short time later, that day arrived. Oliver was well again and Dr. Losberne drove him to the place where Mr. Brownlow resided. Oliver remembered the name of the street and was filled with anticipation as they neared the house.

"Do you remember the place?" asked the doctor.

"It's that one," replied Oliver, all excited. "It's the white house!" he exclaimed.

Alas! When they reached the house, it was empty. A single note on the front door read, "To Let."

On enquiring with the neighbors, they found that Mr. Brownlow and Mrs. Bedwin had, for unknown reasons, moved to the West Indies about six weeks ago.

Oliver was very disappointed. Throughout his sickness, he had hoped that he would see his benefactor again and clear himself of his guilt. But now that was impossible. The thought that the people whom he had loved so, Mr. Brownlow and Mrs. Bedwin, would only remember him as a robber was too much for him to bear. The two returned home sorrowfully.

O LET

Within a fortnight, Mrs. Maylie and Rose took Oliver with them to the country to spend the summer there. It was a new life for Oliver. He enjoyed the clear skies, the woods, and the glistening water, along with the long walks through the fields. In the mornings he visited an old gentleman who taught him how to read and write. Rose also gave him school lessons. He even earned his keep, not by pickpocketing, robbing or cheating, but by looking after the garden every afternoon. Three happy months in the country soon glided away.

One day, Rose suddenly fell sick with a fever. Mrs. Maylie asked Oliver to go into town and fetch the doctor immediately. Worried and anxious about Rose, Oliver ran for almost five miles across the fields till he reached the town. After informing the doctor about Rose's illness he began his journey home.

All of a sudden, he ran into a man who was wearing a black coat. The man glared at him and shouted angrily, "Curse upon your head and death upon your heart, you imp."

He walked towards Oliver and was about to hit him but stumbled and fell to the ground.

Oliver was confused. Who was this man? He glared at

him, but suddenly remembering Rose and the errand he had been sent on, he left the man and ran back home.

The man himself had been shocked to see the boy. He had recognized him and was already planning their next meeting.

Oliver would spend a lot of time reading and looking out of the window of a small room on the ground floor at the back of the house.

One day, after he had been reading for a while, he fell asleep at the window. He dreamt he was back in Fagin's house. Fagin was staring at him and speaking softly to another man.

"Hush, my dear!" he heard Fagin say. "It is certainly him. Let us go away!"

"Without a doubt!" replied the other man. "Do you think I could be mistaken?

Oliver woke up suddenly in shock and fear. As he looked through the window, he saw Fagin and another man. They disappeared in an instant, but the two men had recognized Oliver, and Oliver had recognized them.

For a moment he was stunned. Then he yelled for help. Hearing his cries, the people of the house rushed into the room. They found him looking pale and agitated.

He kept pointing in the direction of the fields shouting, "Fagin! Fagin!"

They hurried out of the house and searched around, but saw no one. They asked him if he was sure he had seen them going that way and he said, "Yes, I'm certain."

Fagin crept through the gap, the other man climbed over the hedge. The doctor believed Oliver's story. But neither the men nor their footsteps were seen by anyone. The mysterious happening was soon forgotten.

Chapter 17

Mysterious Monks Returns

Mr. Bumble sat quietly in a public house sipping his drink and reading the newspaper. He looked unhappy. It was about two months since he had gotten married, but it seemed like ages. He thought back to the time when he was master of all—in the workhouse and his own master. Unfortunately, now things had changed.

All of a sudden, he noticed a familiar face in the public house. The man was the only other customer around, and he kept staring at Mr. Bumble. Finally, in a deep rough voice he spoke to Mr. Bumble. "I recognize you. Weren't you the beadle here once?" he enquired.

"Yes, that's true," replied Mr. Bumble, surprised that he seemed to know him.

"And now?" asked the man.

"Well, I'm master of the workhouse," replied Mr. Bumble proudly.

"Married?" asked the man.

"Yes, just recently, to the workhouse matron," replied Mr. Bumble.

"I guess a married man wouldn't mind earning an honest penny when he could, would he?" asked the man.

"A master of a workhouse most certainly can't afford to refuse a few extra pennies that may come his way," said Mr. Bumble, smiling.

"That's true," said the man putting his hand into his pocket and taking out two gold coins which he handed over to Mr. Bumble. Mr. Bumble looked at them astonished but quickly slid them into his pocket.

"Well," said Mr. Bumble, "now tell me, how can I help you?"

The man told him that he had been looking for Mr. Bumble for some time and then proceeded to question him about Oliver Twist. He wanted him to go back twelve years, to the workhouse and the poor woman who had given birth to him. He asked if he could remember the nurse who had delivered Oliver.

"Yes, I do," said Mr. Bumble. "Unfortunately, she died last winter." The man glared at him. Mr. Bumble remembered the story his wife had told him. It was the night she had agreed to marry him. He realized this was

just the chance for him to make some more money. He then informed the man that although the nurse had passed away, he knew someone who had been with the nurse when she died.

"You must help me find her," said the man anxiously.

"You will have to meet her only through me," said Mr. Bumble.

"When can I meet her?" asked the man, quite excited with this bit of news.

He planned to meet Mr. Bumble the next evening at nine. He wrote an address on a paper and gave it to Mr. Bumble.

Paying his bill, he walked away hastily.

Mr. Bumble stared at the paper. Finding no name on it he ran behind the man and enquired, "Whom should I ask for?"

"Monks," replied the man, "and make sure you keep it a secret!"

Then, he left in a hurry.

The next evening was dull and overcast. As Mr. and Mrs. Bumble set out, it began to rain and it looked like a violent thunderstorm was on its way.

They slowly walked away from the main street, and turned towards a little colony of broken down houses, at a distance of about a mile-and a-half from the town. The colony was built on a swamp, very close to the river.

The couple were both wearing old and shabby outer garments. These served a double purpose; protecting them from the rain, and sheltering them from being observed by others. Mr. Bumble was holding a lantern from which no light shone. He was walking a few steps ahead of Mrs. Bumble. They walked on in total silence. Every now and then, Mr. Bumble slowed down his pace, and looked behind to make sure that his wife was following. When he found her, he continued walking towards their destination.

This was certainly not a good locality towards which they were heading, and people seldom went that way. The inhabitants were mainly ruffians; their main occupations being robbery and crime. The colony was a collection of rundown houses, built with loose bricks and old ship-timber. There were no proper arrangements; the huts were all jumbled together, within a few feet of the riverbank.

Mr. and Mrs. Bumble saw a few leaky boats drawn up on the mud and tied to the small wall which surrounded it. Oars, planks of wood, coils of rope, were lying all around.

Close to the river, in between the cluster of huts, stood a large building. It may have once been a factory, but it had long since gone to ruin. The weather and water seemed to have weakened and rotted the foundation on which it stood. A large portion of the building had already sunk into the water.

It was in front of this wreck of a building that Mr. and Mrs. Bumble stopped. They could hear loud claps of thunder, and the rain continued to pour down violently.

Looking at the scrap of paper he held in his hand Mr. Bumble said, "The place must be somewhere here."

Then he shouted in a loud voice, "Hello, is anyone around?"

"Hello there! Wait a minute, I'll be with you soon," called back a voice from above.

Mr. Bumble looked up and saw a man looking out from the second floor.

He disappeared, and the door closed.

"Is that the man?" asked Mrs. Bumble.

"Yes, yes, it is," replied Mr. Bumble.

Monks opened a small door, near which they stood, and called them in.

They went up a ladder to another floor.

"Now," said Monks to Mrs. Bumble once the three had seated themselves, "is it true that you were with the old woman the night she passed away, and that she whispered a secret to you about something?"

"You mean something about the mother of the boy?" asked Mrs. Bumble. "Yes, indeed."

"My first question to you, then, is what did she say?" asked Monks.

"That, sir, is the second question," replied Mrs. Bumble. "The first question is how much is this information worth?"

"How on earth can I tell you that without knowing what the information is?" said Monks angrily. "It could be worth nothing, or it could be worth twenty pounds. But first you need to tell me all that you know."

"Then add another five pounds! Give me twenty-five pounds in gold, and I'll give you all the information that I have. Nothing before that!" said Mrs. Bumble.

"But what if I'm paying you for nothing?" asked Monks impatiently.

"In that case, you can take back the money. I am after all only a woman, alone and unprotected," said Mrs. Bumble.

"You are certainly not alone, my dear, neither are you unprotected. Am I not with you?" came the quick but hesitant reply from Mr. Bumble.

"You are a fool, so you better keep quiet," replied Mrs. Bumble.

Monks put his hand into his pocket and took out a small canvas bag. From it he counted out twenty-five coins and handed them over to Mrs. Bumble.

"Now," said he, "can you please go on with your story?"

Mrs. Bumble then told Monks how when Sally was dying, she told her of a young woman who had given birth to a child some years ago. The child's mother had given her something and begged of her to keep it safe for her child's sake. But the moment the young woman died, Sally stole it.

"Tell me," cried Monks, now excited, "what did she do with it? Where is it? Whom did she give it to? When?"

"Before she could tell me anymore, she died," said Mrs. Bumble.

"That's not true. You are a liar! Tell me this moment, what else did she say?" asked Monks, so angry he was almost yelling at her.

"I promise you, she didn't say another word, but she was holding on to a scrap of paper," said Mrs. Bumble.

"Was anything written on the paper?" asked Monks.

"Nothing. It was a pawnbroker's duplicate. She may have pawned it and was only able to pay the pawnbroker's interest each year to prevent it from running out. She died with the piece of paper in her hand. It had to be redeemed

in two days. I thought to myself someday something might come of it," said Mrs. Bumble.

"And?" said Monks.

"I redeemed it," said Mrs. Bumble.

"Where is it? What have you done with it?" demanded Monks.

"Here," said Mrs. Bumble, glad to be relieved of the burden. She threw a small leather bag onto the table. Monks pounced on it and tore into it with trembling hands. He pulled out a locket, two strands of hair and a plain gold wedding ring. The ring had the word "Agnes" engraved on it.

"Is this all?" asked Monks.

"Yes, yes it is. Is it what you expected?" asked Mrs. Bumble.

"Yes, it is," said Monks.

"And now that you have found it, what will you do with it? Will you use it against me?" inquired Mrs. Bumble.

"Certainly not! Not against me either. See what I plan to do with it," said Monks.

He then pushed the table aside and pulled at an iron ring on the floor that opened a large trap-door. The door opened so close to Mr. Bumble's feet that he jumped aside with great fear.

"Don't be frightened, look down," said Monks as he lowered his lamp through the door. Mrs. Bumble was brave enough to go to the edge. She looked down and saw the rushing water that ran beneath the mill. Mr. Bumble followed. He looked in fear at the flowing water that was rushing past because of the heavy rain.

Monks very quickly put the locket and other things back into the bag, tied a weight to it and flung it down into the gushing water. It hit the water with a splash and disappeared.

"Make sure you don't mention anything about what happened today," threatened Monks. "And now you may leave. Quickly!"

Mr. and Mrs. Bumble were glad to leave. They climbed down the steps in silence and were soon out into the dark, rainy night.

In the meantime, Bill Sikes had moved all his possessions to a new location. The next evening when he woke up from his sleep, he watched Nancy sitting by the window, stitching.

It was after seven, and when Nancy asked him how he felt he said, "As weak as water!" He asked Nancy to help him sit up on the bed.

Fagin suddenly walked in followed by the Dodger and Charley Bates.

"Do you realize that you haven't come to see me for three weeks? I have been very sick and could have died!" Sikes cried.

"Well Bill," said Fagin, "try not to forget that I was responsible for giving you Nancy to take care of you."

"That's okay, but I still need money to survive," said Sikes.

"I don't have a single penny," said Fagin.

"That's not true. I'm certain you have plenty of money at home. Bring it to me, I need some fast," said Sikes.

"I'll send the Dodger to get it," replied Fagin resignedly.

"I think it's better that you take Nancy with you to fetch it," said Sikes.

After much discussion and bargaining, they decided on a sum of money that was more or less similar to what Sikes had demanded. Fagin then left with the two boys and Nancy.

Once they were back home, Fagin sent the two boys to sleep. He was about to get the money ready for Nancy when there was a knock at the door. It was Monks, who was surprised to see Nancy there.

"Don't worry," said Fagin, "she is just one of my young people. Do you have any good news for me?"

"We need to speak," said Monks.

Fagin knew that Monks did not want to talk to him in front of Nancy, so he took him upstairs to speak to him privately.

Nancy took off her shoes and silently followed them up the stairs. She listened to them speaking from the other side of the closed door. She was very upset with what she heard, especially the words, "The only proof of the boy's identity lies at the bottom of the river."

When she knew the conversation was almost over, she quietly came downstairs.

Monks left immediately after.

Fagin found Nancy looking very pale, but she blamed it on the airless room. He then counted out Sikes' money and gave it to her.

Once Nancy was outside, she sat for a while on the doorstep. She just couldn't go on. All of a sudden, she got up and began to run in the opposite direction, away from Sikes' house. Tears were rolling down her cheeks. Realizing after some time that her situation was hopeless, she stopped running.

Sadly, she turned back and made her way towards Sikes' house.

Chapter 18

When Nancy Met Rose

The next evening as Sikes was staring at Nancy, he found something strange. She didn't look well at all; in fact, she looked as pale as death. When he questioned her about what the matter was, she simply replied, "Nothing."

Since it was time for him to go to bed, he asked her for his medicine. With her back towards him, she poured out a glass of medicine mixed with a small amount of sleeping potion. She then held the glass to his mouth till he had finished it all.

Sikes lay down on his bed and within a short while he was fast asleep. Nancy was sure the drug had taken effect, but she also hoped that she was not too late for what she planned to do.

Putting on her hat and her scarf she silently left the room and set out towards the West End of London. At around ten, she reached a small hotel where the Maylies were staying. She had heard Monks mention that it was near Hyde Park. She waited for a while, and then went in.

She was greeted by a smartly dressed maid who asked her what she wanted.

"I am here to see Miss Maylie," replied Nancy.

The maid was not very happy with the way Nancy was dressed in shabby clothes and so called out to a man for help. The man in turn tried to convince Nancy to leave the hotel.

"Please!" begged Nancy. "Please, will someone at least take a message from me to Miss Maylie?"

After several tries, she managed to convince another house maid to deliver her message to Miss Maylie.

The message was simple.

A young woman wanted to speak to Miss Maylie, but she had to be alone.

The messenger soon returned. He asked Nancy to follow him into a small room, then left her there. Nancy had spent her entire life on the streets. In spite of this there existed within her two qualities: humanity and kindness.

A sweet young lady walked into the room. "I am Miss Maylie, you wanted to see me?" asked Rose in a gentle voice. Nancy was surprised by the gentleness of this beautiful lady.

"If only there were more people like you in the world, there would be fewer people like me," said Nancy.

"Come," said Rose, "sit down, and tell me what troubles you. I will do all I can to help you."

"I will stand," said Nancy, almost in tears, "but please don't speak to me so kindly till you hear what I have to tell you. Can anyone else hear us?"

"No, but why?" asked a puzzled Rose.

"Because," continued Nancy, "I am about to put my life and the lives of many others in your hands. Has Oliver ever told you the story about the night he left Mr. Brownlow and was dragged away by a girl? I am that girl who dragged him away and returned him to Fagin."

"Was it really you?" Rose asked, shocked.

"Yes, I am telling the truth. I live among thieves. I have just run away from these cruel men who will have me murdered if they know I am telling you this story," replied Nancy.

"I am so sorry, your story breaks my heart."

"God bless you for your kindness. Have you heard of a man called Monks?" continued Nancy.

"Never heard of him."

"He knows you and knows that you are here, that's how I found you," whispered Nancy.

Rose was shocked to hear this news.

"A little after Oliver came to live with you, following the robbery, I overheard Monks speaking to Fagin. He had recognized Oliver as the boy he was looking for. They made a plan that if they did find Oliver, Fagin would give him some money. If he took Oliver back to work and made him a thief, he would get more money."

"But what was the reason for this plan?" asked Rose.

"I really don't know," replied Nancy. "It wasn't possible for me to hear anymore. Monks suddenly saw my shadow and I had to run away. I didn't see him again. Then suddenly he appeared last night at Fagin's house. I again listened silently to their conversation. They didn't know I was there. I overheard Monks say that the only proof of the boy's identity now lies at the bottom of a river. The old woman who had stolen the ring and the box was dead. Monks also said that he had the young devil's money. As the two of them laughed and talked he even mentioned a will, it was Oliver's father's will."

"I don't understand all this," said a confused Rose.

"Monks then said that if he could, he would have liked to kill Oliver, but since he was afraid that he would be caught and hanged for the same, he would watch him carefully for the rest of his life. He would make sure that

Oliver never found out the secrets of his past life. He then told Fagin that of all the terrible things Fagin had done to Oliver, nothing would be worse than what he, Monks, would do to his brother Oliver."

"His brother?!" cried Rose.

"Those were his very words," said Nancy. "Be careful, they intend to get him back."

Since it was getting late, she rose from her chair to leave. "I must go," she said, "before they notice I'm missing."

"But, now that you have given me all this information, what should I do? How can I help the poor boy?" asked Rose.

"Find someone who you can trust with this secret. Ask them for advice," said Nancy.

"And if I need you again, where will I find you?" asked Rose.

"Promise me first that you will keep my secret and come to meet me alone, or with the person with whom you decide to share the secret. Besides that no one should watch me, and neither should I be followed," said Nancy.

"I promise," said Rose.

"Very well," said Nancy, "if I am still alive, every Sunday night from eleven till the stroke of midnight, I will walk on the London Bridge." She then left the room in a great hurry.

That night Rose could not sleep. She was anxious about who she should share Nancy's secret with.

The next morning, as she was considering what she should do, Oliver, who had gone out with Mr. Giles, bolted into the room.

"I have seen him, I have seen him! Now, finally, the truth will be revealed," cried Oliver breathlessly.

"Seen whom? Whom have you seen? What has happened? I have always believed you told me the truth," said Rose slowly trying to calm down the boy.

"Mr. Brownlow! The kind gentleman whom I spoke to you about," Oliver almost yelled.

"And where, may I ask, did you see him?" asked Rose.

"He was getting out of a coach. I was trembling so, I couldn't speak to him. I saw him enter a house. Mr. Giles asked around and found out that he lives there. I have written down the address. Here it is!" said an excited Oliver.

Rose took the piece of paper and read the address. Still trying to calm Oliver down, she asked them to get the coach, as she had decided to take Oliver there herself. She then informed her aunt that she was going out for an hour.

As the two of them traveled along Rose was soon

able to track down Mr. Brownlow's house. She asked Oliver to remain in the coach, as she wanted to meet Mr. Brownlow and prepare him before he received Oliver.

She took out a visiting card and presented it to the servant, asking to see Mr. Brownlow immediately.

Very soon she was presented to Mr. Brownlow. He was an old gentleman who looked very kind. Beside him sat another gentleman who did not appear as kind as Mr. Brownlow.

"So, you are Mr. Brownlow?" asked Rose.

"That's true. And this here is my good friend Mr. Grimwig," said Mr. Brownlow.

"I am about to surprise you, I have no doubt, with what I intend to tell you," said Rose. "You had once showed great kindness to a mutual friend. I am sure you will be delighted to hear of him again," she said.

"Indeed! May I ask his name?" asked Mr. Brownlow.

"It is Oliver!" said Rose.

"Do me a favor, and do not mention the kindness and goodness you speak of. If you do have anything to say that will change the bad opinion I have of the boy, please let me know what it is immediately," said Mr. Brownlow.

"A bad one! A very bad one! I'll eat my hat if he is not

a bad one," growled Mr. Grimwig.

"He is a warm-hearted, noble child," said Rose defensively.

"Do not pay attention to my friend. He does not mean what he says. But, tell me more. What do you know about Oliver?" asked Mr. Brownlow.

Rose began her story. She told them everything that had happened to him from the moment he left Mr. Brownlow's house. She only left out the information about Nancy. She concluded by telling him that all Oliver had wished for in these last couple of months was to meet his benefactor and friend.

"This news brings great happiness to me. Where is the boy? Where is Oliver? Why didn't you bring him along with you?" cried Mr. Brownlow.

"He is waiting in the coach outside," said Rose.

Mr. Brownlow hurried to the coach. The moment Oliver saw him he flew into his arms. Mr. Brownlow held his hand and brought him into the house to his room.

"There is one person whom we cannot forget and who will be delighted to see Oliver," said Mr. Brownlow. He then sent for Mrs. Bedwin, his longtime housekeeper.

The old lady soon appeared at the door, curtsied and waited for Mr. Brownlow's orders. As she looked for her spectacles, Oliver grew impatient and ran into her arms crying, "My dear old nurse!"

"God, be kind to me!" she exclaimed. "It is my boy, my innocent boy. I was always certain that he would come back. How good he looks! Dressed like a gentleman's son."

Leaving Oliver and Mrs. Bedwin together, Mr. Brownlow and Rose went to another room where she discussed in full detail the recent events and her meeting with Nancy.

That same evening, they met again at the hotel. This time, Dr. Losberne and Mrs. Maylie were there too.

"It is quite clear that unless we catch Monks and bring him to his knees, it will be very difficult for us to solve this mystery," said Mr. Brownlow. "For that, we need the help of Nancy. She is the only one who can lead us to this strange Mr. Monks. But today is Tuesday, and we cannot do anything till Sunday. Till then, we must wait in silence and not whisper a word to anyone—not even Oliver."

On the very same night that Nancy had escaped from Sikes and gone to meet Rose, a couple was traveling along the road to London. They were Noah Claypole and his girlfriend Charlotte. Noah was the jealous boy who had once bullied Oliver about his dead mother. The two of them were heading for a new life. Charlotte wanted to be a proper lady and Noah a proper gentleman.

"And where should we stop for the night, Noah?" asked a tired Charlotte.

"How would I know?" answered Noah. He too was very tired after the long travel.

"I hope we are at least near," said Charlotte.

"I'm not too sure. But one thing I'm certain about is that we shouldn't stop at the first inn. If Sowerberry decides to follow us, he will definitely find us, and we will have to return with him. I would rather hide in the narrowest streets that I can find. If I hadn't rescued you, you would be in the lock up by now," replied Noah.

"And you would be locked up with me," cried Charlotte.

"Wasn't it you who stole the money from the till?" asked Noah.

"But I took it for you, my dear," replied Charlotte.

"If it was for me, why haven't you given it to me?" asked Noah.

He said this, although he knew very well that he had left the money with her only to appear innocent if they were caught.

They continued walking through the streets of the city, till they came to a tavern. It was no better than the ones that they had seen before.

"I think we should stay here," said Noah. "What is the

name?"

"Three Cripples," said Charlotte.

They pushed open the door and went in.

Fagin was seated in a back room, and he watched them as they ordered their meal.

"That fellow could certainly be of use to me," he thought. He moved a little closer to hear the conversation between the couple.

"We won't have to deal with coffins anymore," said Noah. "I will now have a gentleman's life and you, Charlotte, shall be a lady."

Fagin decided that it was time for him to offer his services to this gentleman-to-be.

"Good evening sir," said Fagin. "Are you from the country?"

"How did you know that?" asked a puzzled Noah.

"The dust on your shoes! We certainly don't have as much dust in London. Wait, let me buy you a drink," said Fagin.

When the drinks arrived, Noah sipped it and said it was good stuff. Fagin then explained to the couple that if they wanted to have a drink like this regularly, they would probably have to rob a till, a pocket or even a bank.

Hearing the word "till", Noah went pale.

"Don't worry about what I said," continued Fagin. "You

are lucky it was only me who overheard your conversation. I am in the same business you speak of. I also have a friend who I think could help you out. You can take up whatever offer he makes. He might even be willing to teach you some of his business later."

"Are you serious?" asked Noah, now interested in the conversation.

"Why wouldn't I be ?" inquired Fagin. "But wait, let me speak to you outside."

"There's no need to take the trouble to move from here," said Noah, knowing that Fagin did not want to continue the conversation in front of Charlotte.

"Charlotte, will you take the luggage upstairs?" asked Noah.

Charlotte agreed, and soon made her way out with the bundles, while Noah held the door open for her.

"Perhaps you could do some tasks for us. Would you be interested in spying?"asked Fagin.

"What are the wages you offer?" asked Noah, with a worried expression on his face.

"Half of what you, my gentleman, and she earns," said Fagin.

Noah was frightened. He now realized that the man had listened to their entire conversation. If they refused his offer, he could hand them over to the police.

"Well," said Noah, "I think I could turn my hand to that and accept your offer."

And so he agreed to meet Fagin at ten the next morning at his house.

Chapter 19

The Artful Dodger's Trial

When Noah and Charlotte reached Fagin's house the next day, they found him very worried.

"My best man has been taken away from me by the police. He was trying to pick a pocket and was caught. They found a silver snuffbox with him. I promise you that snuffbox belonged to him, but they say they know who the owner is. His trial is today!" cried Fagin.

"And what happens next?" asked Noah.

"If they don't find any more evidence against him, they will set him free. If they do, then he's in for life imprisonment. They'll send him off to Australia. Oh my poor boy, my poor boy, he is worth fifty boxes and I would pay the price of as many to set him free. If only you knew my Dodger," said Fagin.

The discussion was cut short with the arrival of Charley Bates. He had a very grim look upon his face.

"It's all over. They have found the owner of the box," said Charley.

"But then we must find out what happens in court," said Fagin.

"Should I go?" asked Charley.

"Are you crazy? How could you ever think of walking into a place where—no, you can't. I can only lose one good man at a time," said Fagin.

"So then, you plan to go yourself?" asked Charley.

"That's not possible," replied Fagin.

"Then whom do we send? How about him? He's new and not known around here," said Charley holding Noah by the hand.

"Oh, I'm not sure, that's not my kind of business," said Noah nodding his head and slowly backing towards the door.

After some time, with much persuasion from Fagin, and more out of fear of the man, Noah agreed to visit the court house, but on one condition. He would go properly disguised. Fagin very quickly provided him with the new attire. Fagin then explained to him the signs he would need to recognize the Dodger.

Noah followed Charley through dark winding streets to within a short distance of the courthouse. From there he was given directions by Charley on how to reach the courtroom and had to travel on his own.

A large crowd had already collected at the courtroom. Most of them were women. Noah looked around eagerly trying to recognize someone who fit the description given to him by Fagin. Somehow, no one there seemed to resemble him.

After waiting for some time, a new prisoner was brought in. Noah was relieved. This most certainly was him. It had to be him. His big coat sleeves were rolled up as usual, his left hand was in his pocket, and he was holding his hat in his right hand.

In a loud, clear voice the Dodger asked why he had been disgraced in this way and what the reason behind him being taken prisoner was. The jailer asked him to be quiet, but he wouldn't.

"Am I not an Englishman? Don't I have my rights and privileges?" he demanded.

"You'll get your rights," replied the jailer.

"Well," continued the Dodger, "I hope the magistrate does not plan to keep me here for long. I have to attend a meeting with a gentleman. He lives in the city. I am a man who keeps his word, and I'm very punctual with my business matters. He will not wait for me if I'm late. I'm certain about that."

"Silence!" said the jailer.

At that moment one of the magistrates walked in and wanted to know what the case was.

"A pickpocketing case," replied the jailer.

The magistrate wanted to know if the boy had been to the courtroom before.

"He should have been several times, I know him very well, Your Worship," replied the jailer.

"Oh, so you do know me, that surely is an attack on my character, in a way," said the Dodger.

The crowd cheered and laughed while the jailer requested for silence. The clerk then asked if there were any witnesses. The Dodger said that he too wanted to see the witnesses because he was certain there were none.

A policeman stepped forward and explained how he had seen the boy try to pick the pocket of a gentleman, in a crowd. He had taken his handkerchief, but finding it old, he had put it back. The policeman found it the best opportunity to catch the boy and take him into custody. On searching the Dodger they had found the silver snuff box in one of his pockets. The box had the owner's name engraved on it.

"Do you have any questions for this witness?" the magistrate asked the Dodger.

"None," he replied.

"Very well! He has been found guilty. Take him away!"

The Dodger was then led away to his cell by the jailer and the policeman.

Once Noah had seen the Dodger being locked up, he returned to Charley, and the two hurried on to give Fagin the news.

The clock struck eleven. Fagin and Sikes were having a conversation, but they stopped to listen.

"One more hour before midnight. It's a dark night too, ideal for our business," said Sikes.

Nancy was getting ready to meet Rose at the decided location. She was about to put on her hat when Sikes called out, "Nancy, where do you think you are going at this late hour?"

"Not too far," came the hurried reply.

"Is that an answer? You aren't going anywhere. Sit down at once," he commanded.

"But I am. I'm not feeling too well, and I need a breath of fresh air," replied Nancy.

"In that case, you can put your head out of the window," said Sikes.

"That won't be enough," said Nancy, "I need it from the street."

But Sikes pretended not to hear her. He got up, went to the door and removed the key. He then walked up to Nancy, pulled off her hat and threw it down.

"That's it," he said. "Stay quietly where you are!"

Nancy continued to beg. "Please Bill, please let me go, I'll be back in an hour. Let me go for just one hour!"

She sat down on the floor next to the door and refused to get up. She even begged of Fagin to ask Sikes to let her go.

Sikes threatened to set Bull's-eye at her throat if she did not listen.

"What is it? What is it?" he yelled. He then grabbed her hands roughly and shouted, "Get up!"

"No, never! Not unless you let me go," Nancy screamed back.

Sikes was now so angry that he dragged her into a small room. Pushing her onto a chair, he held her there. She kept on begging till the clock struck twelve. Then she gave up the fight.

Seeing Nancy calm again, Fagin decided to leave.

"What could be the matter with her?" he thought. She had been absent-minded lately, and she no longer stole or carried out her routine with the same interest that she had before.

What could she be up to? Why did she want to go out at night at that particular hour? Had she found a new friend? All these thoughts continued to cross his mind as he left the room.

The next morning, Noah arrived at Fagin's house on duty again. Fagin informed him that he wanted to send him on a spying mission. The work had to be carried out with much care and caution.

"I hope it's not to another courthouse or to meet some more jailers?" asked a worried Noah.

"No dangers at all in this mission, nothing at all," said Fagin. "It's simple, you need to follow a woman."

"And who is this woman?" questioned Noah.

"Oh, she's just one of us," replied Fagin.

"She has made some new acquaintances, and I have to find out who they are," said Fagin.

"Where do I have to follow her from? Where should I wait for her?" asked Noah.

"All that later, Noah. I'll show her to you at the right time. For now, I just need to know that you will carry out the work. Stay ready!"

It was Sunday night when Fagin spoke to Noah, "The woman you must follow is going out tonight. Come along with me."

Noah followed Fagin through the winding narrow streets till they reached the public house where he and Fagin had first met. He whistled and the door was opened.

Fagin showed Noah a small window. When he looked through, he saw a woman in the other room.

"Is that the one I need to follow? I can't see her face clearly," he said.

"Wait until you can," said Fagin.

When Noah was certain that he would be able to identify the woman, he got down.

In a short while the door opened, and Nancy stepped out. Fagin and Noah hid behind a curtain till she left. It was a dark night when Noah darted out behind her and followed her by the light of the street lamps.

Chapter 20

Goodbye Nancy

The church bell struck a quarter to midnight when Nancy slunk towards London Bridge. Noah was following her in the shadows. When she reached the center of the bridge she stopped. She kept looking around until she heard the bell of St. Paul's strike midnight.

All of a sudden, she heard the sound of a carriage stopping near the end of the bridge.

Noah watched as a gray-haired gentleman and a young lady emerged from it. After paying the driver, they walked towards the bridge.

Nancy walked quickly towards them.

"We must not speak here," she whispered. "Let us get off this public road and go towards the bank of the river."

She then pointed to the steps. The trio went down the steps towards the river.

"I think this is far enough. Can you tell us why you

have brought us to this place? Why not where there is a little light?" said the elderly gentleman. He was none other than Mr. Brownlow. The young lady was Rose Maylie.

Noah slowly crept up and hid behind a pillar a short distance from where they spoke.

"I was scared to speak to you there, someone may see us," whispered Nancy. "In fact I have such a fear in me tonight, I can hardly stand."

"And what, may I ask, are you so frightened of?" asked the elderly gentleman.

"I feel like the shadow of death is following me," replied Nancy.

"Now tell me, why didn't you come to see us last Sunday?" asked the gentleman.

"I tried, but I was held by force. I even tried to put a sleeping pill in his drink, but I still couldn't get away," replied Nancy, scared.

"Very well, you must listen carefully to me. Rose has told me everything that you told her. We have decided to get the secret, whatever it is, from this man you call Monks," said the gentleman. "But, if we can't get him, or we cannot get the secret, then you must take us to Fagin."

"Although Fagin is quite the devil," said Nancy, "I

cannot give him away. He has led a bad life, that's for certain, but so have I. I cannot and will not betray Fagin."

"Then deliver Monks to us, and we will deal with him," said the gentleman.

"But what if Monk finds out that it was me who gave you all the information?" asked Nancy.

"He never will, that I promise," said the elderly gentleman.

Nancy told them where they could find the mysterious Monks. She described the public house that he went to and the day, as well as the time, that he was most likely to be there.

She gave them all this information in whispers. Noah found it impossible to hear most of what she said.

Next, she gave them a description of him.

"Quite tall," she said, "with eyes that are sunken deep into his head. His face is dark like his hair and eyes, and he has an unusual habit of biting his own lip. He walks with a limp and keeps looking over his shoulder. He should be around twenty-eight years of age but appears very old."

The man's face suddenly seemed to show some recognition.

"Does he have any scars?" he asked.

"Why yes, on his throat," said Nancy.

"Is it a burn mark or a scar?" asked the gentleman.

"What's this? Are you telling me you know this man?" cried Nancy, a bit shaken.

Rose also seemed surprised with this last bit of information.

"I think I may know him," said the gentleman as though a piece of a very difficult puzzle had just fallen into place.

"You have really been of great help young lady. How can I repay you for this information?" asked the gentleman.

"You can't," said Nancy, "I am beyond saving!"

"You must not say things like that. Look to the future with hope, not towards the past with a sense of waste," said Rose.

"I have gone too far, there's no turning back. I must go home now. Let me go before someone sees us, let me go," said Nancy sadly.

"But, will you at least take this money?" asked Rose.

"No, I can't. I have not done this for money. However, if you still wish to, give me something that I can remember you by, sweet lady," said Nancy.

"Very well," said Rose, "you can have my handkerchief." She and the gentleman then left. Nancy sat down on the steps and cried. Then she very slowly climbed the steps to the street and disappeared into the night.

Noah stayed in his place for some minutes. Once he was certain that there was no one around, he got out from his hiding place and quickly headed towards Fagin's house. There he reported the conversation that he had managed to hear.

Just before sunrise, Fagin sat on his bed. His mind raced. He was so pale; he looked more dead than alive. He kept thinking of Nancy's betrayal and his lost chance at getting back at Sikes. But most of all, he was frightened that he could be hung for all the information Nancy had given out.

Noah was fast asleep in one corner of the room.

The bell rang, and he slowly climbed the stairs to open it. He returned with Sikes.

He handed over a bundle to Fagin and told him to take care of it as he had gone through enough trouble to get it. Fagin picked up the bundle and locked it in the cupboard. Then, he sat down. His lips were trembling, and his eyes were bloodshot. He kept staring at Sikes.

"Why are you looking at me like that?" asked Sikes.

Fagin raised his right hand and shook his finger, but he could not say a word.

He then bent down and tried to wake Noah up.

"The poor lad is very tired. He's been watching her for a long time," said Fagin.

"Watching who? I don't understand who you are talking about," said Sikes, feeling very confused.

Fagin nudged Noah again, and slowly pulled him into a sitting position. Noah finally woke up, yawned and very sleepily looked around the room.

"Noah, please can you tell this man the story you just told me...about Nancy," said Fagin, holding on to Sikes' hand very tightly, hoping he would not leave before he heard the entire story.

"Where did you say you followed her? To London Bridge, where she met two people?"

"Yes, she did."

"So she met an elderly gentleman and young lady whom you say she has met before?" shouted Fagin. "And they asked her to tell them about her friends and to describe Monks and the place to meet him. She told them everything, is that right?"

"Yes," said Noah, "that's just what she said."

Bill Sikes kept listening and his face grew darker.

"She told them that she could not meet them last Sunday because Bill had forced her to stay at home. He always wanted to know where she was going. The first time she had to go visit the lady, she had given him something to put him to sleep!"

Hearing that Nancy had actually slipped him a sleeping drug made Sikes mad with anger.

"Please Bill," cried Fagin, "please don't be too violent with her."

But Sikes was not listening to him. He rushed out of the room shouting, "Hell's fire!"

He ran through the streets of London straight to his house. He shut the door very quietly and placed a table in front of it. Then he crept up the stairs.

Nancy was fast asleep when Sikes entered the room. "Get up!" he yelled, his voice filled with anger and hate.

"Bill!" cried Nancy. "Why are you looking at me like that?"

He dragged her to the center of the room. "Bill," she pleaded, "what have I done, please, please tell me."

"You were followed and watched and every word you uttered has been heard," he yelled.

"Then please, spare my life," Nancy begged. "I have never betrayed you," she cried holding on to him tight. "Please Bill, don't kill me. I spoke to those people only because they can help us leave this place and start a new life. I promise, I will speak to them again and they will

save us."

With one sudden pull, Sikes freed his arm from her. Then he picked up his pistol. He was about to fire at her but realized if he did the shots would be heard and he would be caught.

So with all his fury he hit her twice.

Nancy fell over, blinded by the blood that was pouring out from her forehead. Pulling out the handkerchief given to her by Rose, she breathed a prayer of mercy to her Maker.

Not satisfied, Sikes seized a heavy club and struck her. The shadow of death that had been following her now possessed her.

Sikes didn't move from the spot for hours. He sat staring at Nancy's dead body for a long time.

Then he got up, lit a fire and threw the club into it. He then washed his clothes, took the dog, locked the door, and left.

Chapter 21

The Meeting

Meanwhile, it was quite late in the evening when Mr. Brownlow stepped out of his carriage at his front door. He gave a signal to two burly-looking men, who stepped out behind him and escorted another man out of the carriage. It was Monks.

When they entered the house, Monks stopped. He was reluctant to go further, and the escorts looked towards Mr. Brownlow for instructions.

"He knows what the alternatives are," said Mr. Brownlow in a stern voice. "If he hesitates, tries to flee, or even lifts a finger against you, drag him into the street and call for the police. I will have him immediately charged and arrested for fraud and robbery."

"How dare you speak to me like this?" shouted Monks. "Who has given you the permission to kidnap me and bring me here?"

"I have," replied Mr. Brownlow. "If you have any problem, go and speak to the police. If you don't, just sit there quietly."

Monks continued to look at Mr. Brownlow's face angrily. After a while, when he had weighed his options, he went and sat down.

"This is fine treatment that I seem to be receiving from my father's oldest friend," he said.

Brownlow turned red in the face.

"It is only because I was your father's oldest friend, my dear man, that I will treat you as kindly as I can, in spite of all the evil that you have done Mr. Monks. Or should I revert to calling you by your proper name, Edward Leeford? You, however, are completely unworthy of that name, and I am happy that you have changed it," he said.

"Well then, can you explain to me what you want from me?" asked Monks.

"I need to speak to you about your brother," said Mr. Brownlow.

"What brother? I do not have any brothers. You know I was an only child," said Monks.

"Don't speak, just listen to what I have to say first. Your parents had an unhappy marriage. It was a marriage filled with hatred for each other. You were the only child from that marriage. They finally separated. Your mother went to live abroad and took you with her. She soon forgot about the marriage, but your father was shattered and could not forget it for many years," said Mr. Brownlow.

"So what happened next?" asked Monks impatiently. He was now determined to hear the whole story.

"After they had been separated for some time," continued Mr. Brownlow, "your father found new friends. Among them was a beautiful girl called Agnes. Your father fell in love with her. She was soon to have his child, but your father was called away to Rome to visit a rich relative who was on his deathbed."

"Does your story have no end?" asked Monks.

"No, there's more. The relative passed away and left a large inheritance to your father. Unfortunately, your father fell ill in Rome. Your mother arrived to see him, with you. But your father was so ill that he died the next day. You and your mother were at his bedside. Before your father left for Rome, he had come to see me."

"I know nothing about what you speak of," said an angry Monks.

"Your manner suggests that you do know something. So let me continue," said Mr. Brownlow. "Your father told me what he wished and gave me some personal items, along with a painting of the girl. He also told me that he planned to give some of his riches to your mother and you, and then leave England with Agnes. The rest of his money had to be transferred to her. That was the last time I saw him. After I heard of his death, I tried my best to find Agnes and her family, but they had left their home. No one knew what had happened to her or where she had disappeared without a trace. And then suddenly, by chance, I found and rescued your poor brother; Oliver Twist. He was sent to me like a miracle, and he was a feeble young soul. As he lay on his bed recovering from a sickness, I was struck with astonishment at the strong resemblance he bore to the portrait.

"But you cannot prove anything against me," shouted Monks.

"That we shall wait and see," continued Mr. Brownlow, "but let me continue. Before I could establish the boy's history, as you know, he was lost."

"How would I know that?" asked Monks.

"Simply, because you were involved in his abduction," replied Mr. Brownlow.

"I dare you to prove anything against me," cried Monks.

Mr. Brownlow went on narrating his story.

"Since your mother was dead, the only way to solve

the mystery was by finding you. I was told that you had traveled to the West Indies with the inheritance. I went there in an attempt to locate you, but in the meantime you had left and were supposedly in London. I returned but was unable to find you till tonight. In the last two weeks I have discovered your story."

"And," sneered Monks, "now that you have found me, now what?"

"You knew all along that you had a brother and also that your father had made a will that provided for the child. However, your mother destroyed the will and left the secret with you on her deathbed."

"Nonsense, this is all nonsense," said Monks.

"There was a reference to a child in the will. So you traveled to the town where your brother was born to find evidence of his birth. There you found the proof of his birth and who his parents were, but you destroyed it. Remember the words of your friend Fagin: the only proof of the boy's identity now lies at the bottom of the river. The old woman who had got the proof from the mother is also dead."

"No!" shouted Monks, shocked to hear the words he had spoken in private, now being repeated back to him.

"Every evil word spoken between you and your partner in crime Fagin is known to me," said Mr. Brownlow. "To add to this, you have also been party to a murder! By revealing your secrets you have indirectly caused the death of another human being."

Monks was shocked with all the accusations being made against him.

"Will you now confess to all your deeds and tell me the whole truth?" asked Mr. Brownlow.

"Yes, yes I will, I have no other choice," said Monks. He slumped into his chair and looked like a beaten man.

"Will you swear in front of witnesses?" asked Mr. Brownlow.

"I promise, I will!" said Monks.

"Besides, you must make amends with your brother by remembering the terms of the will that was destroyed, and you must pay him back what is due to him. Only then will you be free to go."

Whilst Monks was thinking about all that Mr. Brownlow had said, Dr. Losberne entered the room.

"The man shall be arrested tonight," he said.

"You mean the murderer?" cried Mr. Brownlow. "And Fagin? What news of Fagin?"

"When I last heard, he had not yet been taken in, but he should be captured anytime soon," said Dr. Losberne.

"And you Monks, have you decided?" asked Mr.

Brownlow.

"Yes, but will you keep my secret?" asked Monks.

"Very well then, stay here. This is your only hope of safety," said Mr. Brownlow.

Saying that, he left the room with Dr. Losberne, after locking the door behind him.

Chapter 22

Sikes Meets his End

Later that night, in a tavern in East London on the River Thames, a rumor was afloat. Fagin had been arrested.

The name of the tavern was Jacob's Island and the buildings located around it were the poorest on the river. There were no roofs, no glass on the windows and even the walls were crumbling down. The residents who lived there were the ones who needed to hide.

In one such house, three men sat gloomily. They hardly spoke. They were none other than Toby Crackit and two of his companions. Fagin had been arrested that afternoon and was to be hung in six days. Noah had also been arrested and was telling everything to the police.

"And where is Charley?" asked one of the boys.

"He should be here soon. There is nowhere he can go; everyone from the Three Cripples has been arrested."

While they spoke of the arrests, Bull's-eye, Sikes' dog, suddenly bounded into the tavern through the window. The people in the tavern knew what that meant; Sikes would arrive next.

A tapping was heard at the door. Toby Crackit went to the door and returned with a man. He had a handkerchief tied over the lower part of his face. Another handkerchief was tied over his head.

The moment he pulled them off, they saw a face that was the color of ash. The eyes were sunken, and he had a beard that had not been cut for three days. It was Sikes. Pulling up a chair he sat down. No one uttered a word.

Finally, Sikes broke the silence by saying, "Is it true that Fagin has been caught? I read it in tonight's paper."

"It's true."

There was more silence.

"Will someone say something? For God's sake!" shouted Sikes.

The knocking at the door was heard again. Crackit went to open the door and returned with Charley Bates.

"Toby," shouted Charley as he saw Sikes sitting on the chair staring at him, "why didn't you mention to me that he was here?"

"Charley!" said Sikes getting up from his chair and moving towards him.

"Don't you dare come near me, you monster," yelled Charley.

Sikes' eyes sank to the ground.

"Listen, the three of you," continued Charley, getting more and more agitated as he spoke, "I am no longer scared of him. If anyone comes here looking for him, I will give him up. I don't care if he kills me. Even if they said they were going to boil him alive, I would still give him up."

"Murderer! Help!" Charley yelled.

With these cries, he threw himself on Sikes and knocked him to the ground.

"You murderer, you murdered Nancy!" cried Charley. The boy wrestled with the much bigger man on the floor. Sikes however was much stronger and was soon on top of Charley. His knee was on Charley's throat.

All of a sudden, Crackit pulled him back and pointed towards the window. They could see lights and hear the loud thunder of footsteps of the police and citizens coming towards the tavern. There was a loud thumping on the door.

"He's up here! Help!" shouted Charley. "Break open the door!"

Voices from outside shouted, "In the king's name!" and heavy blows were heard on the door below.

"Break down the door!" shouted a desperate Charley. Sikes caught Charley and threw him into a small room, then locked him inside.

"Are you all sure the door downstairs is locked?" shouted Sikes.

"It's double locked and even chained," replied a scared Crackit.

"And how strong are the door panels?" shouted Sikes.

"They are lined with metal."

"The windows, what about the windows? Are they lined too?" he yelled again.

"Yes!"

Sikes then threw open one of the windows, and shaking his fist at the large crowd gathered below, shouted, "Do your worst, you won't get me!"

The yells from the crowd would not stop. They grew louder and louder. Some wanted to set fire to the building. Others demanded that the police shoot them all dead. There were yells for ladders, others shouted for hammers. Some people were running around desperately with torches, looking for the murderer. All the people were waving their fists and shouting angrily.

Shutting the window again, Sikes suddenly shouted, "The tide! I saw the tide was in as I came upstairs. Give me a rope. All the people and policemen are at the front. I will jump into the water from behind and escape. Fast, get me a rope."

The men immediately pointed to the place where the ropes were kept. Sikes grabbed a long rope and bolted out through a small door that led to the roof. The windows at the back were all bricked up a long time ago. There was just one small window in the room in which Charley had been locked.

Charley yelled out to the people to guard the back.

When they saw Sikes, someone shouted, and they all ran towards the back of the house.

Sikes, in the meantime, walked carefully along the roof and looked over the edge. He was hoping to see the tide. But all he could see was no tide, only mud. The tide was long gone.

The crowd watched him in silence. Realizing that he could do nothing, they began to shout again.

In all this confusion, word spread that the police and some people had managed to force open the door. The crowd now all rushed to the front of the house.

Till now Sikes had tried to hide himself. He was afraid of the people's anger. When he saw them moving away, he was determined to make one last try and jump into the sea of mud.

Putting his foot against the chimney, he desperately tied one end of the rope around it. He made a noose of the other end that could go around him. He planned to slip the loop over his head and under his armpits. He would then leap into the ditch.

His knife was in his hand, ready to cut the rope the moment he reached the ground.

Once he was down in between the noise, darkness and commotion, his plan was to slowly slip away from all his pursuers.

He put the noose around his neck and was about to pass it down around his body, when he was suddenly distracted and staggered by a ghastly sight.

Was it a shout from someone?

Was it the thought of Nancy's glaring eyes?

Throwing his hands up to try to catch the rope, he stumbled. It was too late. He had lost his balance. The noose tightened around his neck, and he tumbled over

the edge of the roof. Down went Sikes. Down, down, down he fell. Then his body stopped. The old chimney shook with the shock but kept standing.

Everything was quiet as the body of Bill Sikes swung lifelessly back and forth above the road.

Chapter 23

Oliver Finds a Relative

It was two days after the death of Bill Sikes. Oliver found himself in a carriage heading towards the town where he was born. He was accompanied by Rose, Mrs. Maylie, Mrs. Bedwin and Dr. Losberne. Their carriage was followed by another one with Mr. Brownlow and Monks.

Oliver was very excited to see all the familiar places as they approached the town. Different emotions flooded through his mind as he remembered his younger days; poor, homeless, wandering about with no one to help him.

They passed the old nursery.

"Look, over there," cried Oliver, holding tightly onto Rose's hand and pointing out of the carriage window. "The very stile that I climbed over. Those are the hedges that I hid behind, for the fear that someone would find me and take me back inside. That's the path through the fields to the old house where I lived as a child."

Oliver suddenly remembered his old friend Dick.

"If only I could meet Dick again," he said.

"You never know, you probably can. Then you can share with him the story of your life and how happy you are now," said Rose. "You can also tell him that you are rich now, and of all your happiness none is greater than coming back to see him, and make him happy too."

"Yes! Can we take him away from this place, get him some new clothes, teach him and then send him off to a place in the country where he can become strong and well again? Please, please can we do this for him?" pleaded Oliver.

Rose nodded yes. Oliver was smiling and there were tears of happiness rolling down his cheeks. She just could not refuse him anything.

In his excitement, Oliver could not stop talking.

"I am certain you will be kind to him, because you are so kind to me, and so kind and good to everyone you meet. I know you will be very sad to hear his story. But it's over now and I'm sure you will smile again. Do you know, when we said goodbye, he said: God bless you. That was the time when I ran away. Now it's my turn to say 'God bless you' to him and show him how I love him and how grateful I am for his blessings."

Sowerberry's shop looked unchanged, though it did appear a little bit smaller than he remembered, and less impressive in its appearance. He kept looking out at all the familiar places of his childhood; the shops, the houses, etc. They all seemed to be connected with some incident in his early years.

They finally stopped in front of the chief hotel. Oliver remembered staring up at the building in awe, thinking it was a huge palace. Its beauty and grandeur seemed to have decreased over the years. Mr. Grimwig was waiting for them there. They entered the hotel and sat down to have dinner. Mr. Brownlow, who had also reached the hotel, sat in a separate room with another man whom Oliver could not see. They were going through some papers together.

At about nine, when dinner was complete, Dr. Losberne and Mr. Grimwig entered the room where Oliver and Rose were seated. Mr. Brownlow and the unknown man followed them. Oliver almost shrieked with fear when he saw the man's face. It was the same man who had frightened him in the market place and the one whom he had seen peering in through the window of his room with Fagin.

"Oliver," said Mr. Brownlow, "this man is your brother."

Monks looked at him with pure hatred, then pulled up a chair and sat down next to the door. Mr. Brownlow walked up to Oliver, holding some papers in his hand.

"This is a really painful job, but it has to be done," said Mr. Brownlow.

"Hurry, continue speaking, you can't keep me here forever," said Monks angrily.

"This boy is your half-brother. He is the child of your father, Mr. Edwin Leeford, who was also my very good friend, and the poor young Agnes Fleming. She died soon after giving birth to him," said Mr. Brownlow.

"All this I am aware of. Besides, you have the story written here," said Monks impatiently. He pointed to the papers that Mr. Brownlow was holding in his hands.

"That's true. I do have a signed confession, but I would also like these good people gathered here to hear the truth from you, directly," said Mr. Brownlow looking around at the small crowd in the room.

"Listen and I will tell you my story," Monks started. "When my father was unwell in Rome, my mother and I went to see him. The day after we arrived, he died. But he had left some papers behind, two of which were addressed to you Mr. Brownlow. Since my mother and I were with him at that time, we opened them. One was a letter to

Agnes, the other was his will."

"And what did the letter say? Can you please tell us?" asked Mr. Brownlow.

"The letter stated that he hoped she would forgive him and not curse him for leaving her alone with the child. He then reminded her of the box with the locket and the ring in it. The ring had the name Agnes engraved on it with a space for the surname which he hoped one day to include," said Monks.

Oliver's eyes were filled with tears hearing this story.

Mr. Brownlow continued with the rest of the story. "The will clearly stated that he was upset with his wife, Monks' mother, and Monks, for all the miseries they had given him in his lifetime. But he still left you a sum of eight hundred pounds each. The rest of his money, along with his property, was left to Agnes and her child. But there was also one more stipulation in the will. If at any time Agnes' child was to fall into any disgrace by any public act of dishonor, he would lose all his inheritance and all the money would go to you, Monks," said Mr. Brownlow.

"My mother, who was so unhappy with the will, did what any woman would have done in her place—she burnt it. She kept the letter along with the other proof," said Monks. "So the letter never reached Agnes. She however mentioned the truth to Agnes' father. He was so upset that he ran away and changed his name. He did not want his friends to find him. He died soon after of a broken heart."

"All these secrets were revealed to me by mother on her deathbed. She was not sure whether Agnes was alive or dead but was convinced that she had a child and it was a boy. I promised her that I would somehow find the boy. I finally did manage to find him. I started off well, and had it not been for gossip, would have completed the job well too," said Monks.

Mr. Brownlow then explained how Monks had presented Fagin with the letter, and they had almost succeeded in making the boy a criminal. Fagin had also received a large reward for holding Oliver a prisoner.

Mr. Brownlow turned to Monks and enquired about the locket and the ring.

Monks told him that he had bought them from the man and woman who had taken them from the old nurse, who in turn had stolen it from the dying Agnes.

Monks gave them all this information without raising his eyes or head. "You know what happened to them," he said.

Mr. Brownlow then nodded to Mr. Grimwig who left

the room, only to return with Mrs. Bumble who was dragging Mrs. Bumble behind her.

"Do my eyes deceive me, or is that really you my little Oliver? If only you knew how sad I've been, how I've missed you, my Oliver, my dearest O-li-ver!" cried Mr. Bumble on entering the room and seeing Oliver there.

"Hold your tongue, you fool, you are only making a fool of yourself," said Mrs. Bumble angrily.

But Mr. Bumble just would not stop.

"Am I not supposed to feel for the boy?" he cried. "I, who brought him up? When I see him sitting between ladies and gentlemen, shouldn't I feel proud? I have always loved him as if he was my own grandfather," he said, a bit confused in all his excitement on seeing the boy.

He asked Oliver if he remembered the good gentleman in the white waistcoat. The man had gone to heaven in an oak coffin with plated handles, Mr. Bumble told Oliver.

At this point Mr. Grimwig stepped forward and asked Mr. Bumble to control his feelings.

"I will do my best," said Mr. Bumble.

"How do you do? I hope you are well, sir," said Mr. Bumble to Mr. Brownlow who had just moved towards the couple.

He then pointed towards Monks and asked the couple,

"Do you know that man?"

"No," replied Mrs. Bumble.

"And you, do you know him?" asked Mr. Brownlow to Mr. Bumble.

"I have never seen him in my life," mumbled Mr. Bumble.

"So you couldn't possibly have sold him anything?" asked Mr. Brownlow.

"Never," replied Mr. Bumble.

"Perhaps, a locket and a gold ring?" continued Mr. Brownlow.

Now Mrs. Bumble was angry. "We told you we haven't," she replied. "Why have you brought us here to ask us all these silly questions?"

At this point Mr. Brownlow again made a sign to Mr. Grimwig who left the room. He returned, this time with two old women from the workhouse who were so weak and skinny they shook and tottered as they entered.

"Do you remember the night old Sally died," said one of the two women to Mrs. Bumble, raising her shriveled hand, "you thought you had closed the door, but you couldn't shut out the sound. Neither could you seal the chinks in the wall."

The other woman looked around and kept saying, "No,

no, you couldn't!"

"We were both listening carefully to your conversation. We could hear the poor girl trying to tell you what she had done. We also saw you taking the paper from her trembling hand. We even followed you to the pawnbroker's shop the next day," said the first woman.

"And, we also know that a locket and gold ring was given to you. We were there, don't you worry, we saw it all," said the second woman.

"Would you now like us to call in the pawnbroker?" asked Mr. Grimwig moving towards the door.

"No, that is not required," replied Mrs. Bumble. "If Monks has been a coward and confessed it all, as I see he has, and these two old hags have told their story, I have nothing more to hide. I did sell them to Monks, and they now lie in a place where you will never be able to get them again. So what if we did, what will you do to us?" asked an angry Mrs. Bumble.

"Nothing for now, except that we will make sure that neither of you is ever again employed in a position of trust. Your employment at the workhouse is now terminated. And now you can leave the room, immediately," said Mr. Brownlow.

"I did nothing; it was all her fault—Mrs. Bumble's. She

was the one to insist that we do it," said a panic-stricken Mr. Bumble. He said this after he had made sure that Mrs. Bumble had left the room.

"That is definitely not an excuse Mr. Bumble," said Mr. Brownlow. "You were present when the jewelry was destroyed, and so you are the guiltier of the two, in the eye of the law. The law will say that your wife acted according to your instructions."

Mr. Bumble had nothing more to say. He put his hat on his head, pushed his hands into his pockets and silently followed his wife down the stairs.

Mr. Brownlow was now at the end of his revelations.

"Give me your hand, young lady," said Mr. Brownlow to Rose. "Do not tremble. There is nothing to fear about what I have to say to you next."

He then turned to Monks and asked, "Do you know this young lady who is here with us today?"

"Yes, I do," said Monks.

"But I have never seen him before," muttered Rose. She could not understand how she could ever be associated with a horrible man like this.

"But," said Monks, "I have seen you often."

"Agnes' father had two daughters," said Mr. Brownlow. "Does anyone know what happened to the other child?"

"When Agnes' father died in a strange land, with a different name, he did not leave a note or even a letter behind. As a result, as much as they tried, no one was able to trace his relatives or any of his friends. The child had to be cared for. The child was then taken away by some poor people who cared for her as their own," said Monks.

"Go on," said Mr. Brownlow.

"My mother tried her best to find Agnes. But she couldn't. She did manage to find Agnes' sister though."

"And did she take the child with her?" asked Mr. Brownlow.

"No she didn't, although she found the child leading a miserable existence with the poor family. She gave them some money to care for the child and promised to return, but never did. A wealthy widowed lady saw the child, took pity on her and decided to care for her. She remained with the lady and was very happy with her. I did not see her again until two or three months ago," said Monks.

"And do you see her now?" asked Mr. Brownlow holding on to Rose's hand.

"Yes," replied Monks, "she is leaning on your arm."

Rose almost fainted, but Mrs. Maylie held on to her.

"Don't worry, my dearest child, you are mine now. I would never let you go away from me for all the treasures in the world," said Mrs. Maylie. "She is my sweet companion, my very own dear girl."

"And you," cried Rose clinging to Mrs. Maylie, "are the only friend I have ever had, the kindest and the best friend! Oh my heart will surely burst. I cannot bear anymore news," Rose said tiredly.

Oliver was astonished with all the news himself. He was related to Rose by blood!

"How can I call you aunt?" cried Oliver, throwing his arms around Rose's neck. "I'll never be able to call her aunt. She will be my sister, my very own sister. The sister that my heart loved so dearly the moment I saw her!"

The two orphans wept as they hugged each other and wiped away each other's tears.

Chapter 24

The End of Fagin

The court was packed with people. They were everywhere. They were all curious and waiting. All eyes were fixed on only one man—Fagin. He seemed to be surrounded by a sea of bright gleaming eyes.

Fagin stood, with one hand resting on the wooden slab that was in front him. The other hand was on his ear. His head was thrust forward, to allow him to hear clearly every word uttered by the judge. He looked anxious at times, but never stirred a hand or foot. In fact, he had hardly moved from the beginning of the trial. Even when the judge had stopped speaking, he continued to gaze at him.

After some time, there was a cry for silence, and everyone looked towards the door. The jury was returning from making their decision.

Fagin stared at their faces but could gather no information from them. They may as well have all been made of stone. The room was silent as the verdict was announced.

There was not a murmur, not a breath, just pin drop silence. "Guilty!"

Fagin was found guilty of many crimes. He was sentenced to death.

The building was filled with shouts, groans and cheers. It sounded almost like thunder. The news spread to the outside. He would be hung by Monday.

After a while the noise subsided. The judge then asked Fagin if there was any reason why the death sentence should not be given to him. All Fagin could reply was that he was an old man, a very old man.

Once in the prison cell, he sat down on a stone bench next to the door. Although at that time it seemed like he could not remember a word, he kept trying to recollect what the judge had said.

It finally came back to him: to be hanged by the neck till he is dead—that was the end.

He kept thinking about all the men he had known in the past who had met with the same end. Many had been hanged because of the information he had given to the authorities.

He had even watched some of them die and made a joke about it. He had laughed because some of them had died with a prayer on their lips.

Strong vigorous men at one moment, and the next they were just a dangling heap of clothes.

He kept thinking. Some of them had most probably lived in the same cell as him.

They may even have sat on the same bench as him. It was very dark in the cell.

"Why couldn't they put in a light?" he wondered. This cell must have been built many years ago, and hundreds of men must have spent their last hours in it.

After some time, when his hands started hurting with all the beating he had done against the door and walls, he saw two men approaching the cell. One was holding a candle in his hand which he placed in an iron candlestick that was fixed on the wall. The other pulled a mattress in for him to sleep at night. The prisoner was not to be left alone anymore.

It was finally night! A dark, miserable, silent night. Most people are glad when they hear the church clock strike. It signifies the coming of a new day. To Fagin, the clock striking signaled despair. The deep hollow boom of the iron bell came to him as the sound of death.

Then day came and it was soon gone. Then night came again. He had hardly spoken to the two men who watched over him one at a time. They too had not made an attempt to talk to him. All he did was sit in his cell, awake but dreaming.

On the day they had captured him, he had been wounded on his head with stones thrown by the crowd. His head was now bandaged with a linen cloth. His long red hair hung down over his pale face. His beard was knotted, and his eyes shone with a strange light in them. His unwashed skin burned with a fever. He looked so terrible, that it was impossible for one man to sit there and keep watch over him alone. The two men now kept watch together.

On the day he was to be hanged he had two visitors.

Mr. Brownlow and Oliver had got special permission from one of the sheriffs to come see him.

"Is the young gentleman with you also going to see the prisoner, sir?" asked the man on duty who was taking them into the cell. "It is certainly not a sight for children, sir," he said.

"I understand, my friend; it is not, but my business with the prisoner is closely connected with the boy, and since the boy has seen him through his good times and bad, I think he needs to see him, even if it causes him some pain," replied Mr. Brownlow.

All this was said at a slight distance from Oliver, so he could hear anything.

The man did not have anything more to say. He looked at Oliver with some curiosity, and then opened a gate and led them on. They followed him through dark winding paths towards the cells.

He finally knocked on one of the doors with his keys. The two attendants came out and asked the visitors to follow the jailer into the cell. Fagin was seated on his bed, rocking himself from side to side. Seeing Mr. Brownlow and Oliver he demanded to know what they wanted.

Mr. Brownlow explained to him that he, Fagin, had some papers which were given to him by a man called Monks for safekeeping.

"That's a lie," shouted Fagin, "a lie! I don't have a single paper with me."

Mr. Brownlow continued, "For the love of God, Fagin, tell me where they are. Don't say you don't have them. You are about to die. Sikes is dead. Monks has confessed. There is no hope now. Where are the papers?"

"Okay," said Fagin. "Oliver, come to me. Come here. Let me whisper to you where the papers are."

Mr. Brownlow hesitated to let Oliver go towards this crazy man.

"I am not frightened of him," said Oliver in a whisper, leaving Mr. Brownlow's hand.

Pulling Oliver towards him Fagin said, "I have kept the papers in a canvas bag, in the top front-room. When you enter, look a little way up the chimney. You will find them there in a small hole. But now, I want to talk to you, my dear Oliver, let me to talk to you."

"Yes," said Oliver, "I will pray with you, let me say a prayer. Will you say just one prayer upon your knees, with me, and we can continue talking till morning?"

Fagin however had another plan in mind. He held on tightly to Oliver. He wanted him to take him outside and somehow let him escape. He was his last hope.

"Outside," he cried, "you can get me out! Take me with you, now!" He kept pushing Oliver forward, towards the door.

Oliver burst into tears and panicked.

"Please dear God!" said Oliver. "Forgive this wretched man!"

But Fagin would not let go of Oliver. He was determined that Oliver would somehow be able to take him out of the door to freedom.

"That way, that way," cried Fagin. "We need to go in that direction. Open this door first. If I start to shake and tremble, as we go past the gallows, don't you worry, just keep moving, just don't stop, hurry, hurry along. Now, right now!"

The jailer, seeing what was happening, was also worried and asked Mr. Brownlow if he had any more questions.

"Nothing more to ask, sir," said Mr. Brownlow.

"Then," said the jailer, "you had better leave him alone."

At that moment the door of the cell opened and Fagin's two attendants returned.

Fagin continued to beg of Oliver to set him free.

"Please Oliver, please Oliver," begged Fagin, "don't leave me here. Let's get out from here. We must make haste. Faster, faster Oliver!"

The two attendants managed to pull Oliver away from Fagin. He struggled desperately for a moment, then let out a desperate cry. The cry was so shrill it seemed to penetrate the massive walls. It followed them, as they went out into the open yard.

Oliver was very disturbed with all that had happened, and he fainted. He was so upset and felt so weak that for almost an hour he had no strength to walk or even take a step.

It was sometime before Mr. Brownlow and Oliver could leave the prison gates.

As they finally emerged, they saw a great crowd had already collected around the gallows. There were people everywhere. They were smoking and playing cards to pass time. The windows were filled with people. This would be the place where later in the day Fagin would be hanged.

AGNES

Chapter 25

A Happy Ending for Oliver

The story finally had a happy ending for Oliver. What happened to the rest can be told in simple but few words.

In less than three months, Rose was married in the village church to Harry Maylie. They had a new home and Mrs. Maylie continued to stay happily with the young couple.

According to the will left by Oliver's father, Oliver was to receive all of his father's property. Mr. Brownlow, however, was a just and honest man. He felt that Monks should be given a chance to change his life and pursue a career. He therefore decided that the property was to be equally divided between the two brothers, and Oliver agreed with him.

Monks took his share of the money and sailed to America. There he quickly squandered it all, and having nothing to fall back on, went back to his old criminal ways.

He was caught and put into prison, where he died. That was the last of Fagin's main gang.

Noah Claypole was granted full pardon because he gave evidence in the trial against Fagin. After some thought, he became a police informer. He and Charlotte remained together. He managed to buy her new respectable clothes, and Noah and she are often seen walking out of church looking like a proper lady and gentleman.

Mr. and Mrs. Bumble lost their jobs at the workhouse. They led a life of misery, became poorer and poorer and finally landed up as paupers, in the very same workhouse that was once ruled by them.

Charley Bates, shocked by the murder of Nancy, decided to lead an honest life once he was out of prison. He worked very hard and became a farmer's helper. He decided that he would collect a lot of money and buy his own farm.

The Artful Dodger was in prison for some time because of theft. He did well in prison and had many friends; from the lowest of inmates right up to the warden himself. Not much is known about his life after he came out of prison, but he was often seen in crowded places and noisy taverns.

Mr. Brownlow adopted Oliver as his son. He, along with Oliver and his old housekeeper, Mrs. Bedwin, moved to the same village as Rose and Mrs. Maylie and bought a house close to them. That was the only wish Oliver had, to live near Rose. Mr. Brownlow kept educating Oliver and telling him stories and grew to love him more and more each day.

As for Rose, she and Oliver grew closer to each other. Their earlier lives and experiences as orphans made them kind, loving and merciful people. They were all finally very happy.

Within the altar of the old village church stands a white marble tablet, which bears but one single word, "Agnes". It is placed there in memory of Oliver's mother. There is no coffin buried there and hopefully no one will have to be buried there for years to come.

Sometimes you will find the two orphans, Rose and Oliver, standing beside it. They are probably reflecting upon those they love dearly—the living and the dead.

Questions

Chapter 1

I. Answer the following questions.

a. What is a workhouse?

b. Describe the mother who gave birth to the little boy.

c. Who were the only people who were present to welcome the baby into the world?

d. What was the mother's dying wish?

e. Which line tells you that the woman died?

II. Find the meaning of the following words and use them in sentences of your own.

a. Dreary b. Orphan

c. Refuge d. Frail

e. Affectionately

III. "Had he known at that moment that he was left an orphan, all alone in the world, to be cared for by the people in the workhouse, he might have cried a little louder." What do you think these lines mean? Explain them in your own words.

Chapter 2

I. Answer the following questions.

a. Who gave Oliver his name? What is a beadle?

b. Mention two adjectives that are used to describe Mr. Bumble.

c. Who took care of Oliver at the nursery? Do you think she was a kind woman? Why?

d. Where was Oliver when Mr. Bumble came to visit him?

e. Why did Mrs. Mann give Oliver something to eat when Mr. Bumble came to take him away?

II. Name the following.

a. Mrs. Mann wiped this from Oliver's face and hands.__________

b. On this birthday of Oliver's Mr. Bumble paid him a visit.________

c. Mr. Bumble used this on any of the children who were naughty.________.

d. The one person who was happy with the situation at the workhouse._____

e. The number of gentlemen seated around the table._______

III. Who said the following to whom?

a. "We must put him to work."

b. "You know you're an orphan, I suppose?"

c. "What's that, sir?"

d. "What are you crying about?"

e. "You will be well educated here."

IV. Now that you have read the chapter, do you know what an orphan is? How, according to you, should an orphan be treated?

Chapter 3

I. Answer the following questions.

a. What is gruel? Where were the meals served?

b. Why did the bowls look so clean after the boys had eaten from them?

c. Why did the boys come up with a plan?

d. What was the punishment Oliver received for asking for more gruel?

e. What did the notice posted outside the workhouse read?

II. Use one adjective from the chapter to describe the following.

a. ________ soup   b. ________ bowl

c. ________ hall   d. ________cook

e. ________ room

III. Find the meaning of the following words and use them in sentences of your own.

a. Torture   b. Reward

c. Chimney-sweep   d. Waistcoat

e. Apprentice

IV. "Please sir, I want some more." List three things that happened after Oliver said these words.

Chapter 4

I. Answer the following questions.

a. Why did Mr. Sowerberry visit the workhouse?

b. Why was Mrs. Sowerberry unhappy when she saw Oliver?

c. Describe Noah Claypole's first meeting with Oliver.

d. How do you know that Charlotte was a kind person?

e. What was the brilliant idea that Mr. Sowerberry came up with to put Oliver to use?

II. Give the meanings of the following phrases:

a. Bag of bones

b. Shocked at his appetite

c. Drew back the bolts

d. Of a broken heart

e. Gave way to his feelings

III. Who said the following to whom?

a. "If you do come back, you will be sent out to sea and drowned."

b. "You don't mind sleeping amongst the coffins, do you?"

c. "She's dead, of a broken heart."

d. "He'll murder me. Help! Help!"

e. "Let me out, let me out!"

IV. "Oliver had a very restless sleep that night." Describe the night.

Chapter 5

I. Answer the following questions.

a. What did Oliver do the next morning?

b. Where did he find himself?

c. Whom did he meet?

d. Describe Dick.

e. What did Dick say to Oliver?

II. Fill in the blanks.

a. Oliver tied up some of his ______ into a little bundle.

b. Looking into the _______, he saw a boy at work.

c. Oliver told Dick that he was running away to seek his ______.

d. Dick climbed up the low ______to give Oliver a hug.

e. Both the boys had spent a lot of time together and had even been beaten and _____ up together several times.

III. Oliver knew he would never forget Dick. In your own words, describe what you thought of the friendship that existed between the two boys.

Chapter 6

I. Answer the following questions.

a. What was Oliver running away from?

b. Where did he finally rest? What did the milestone read?
c. Why did Oliver decide to run away to the city of London?
d. Describe the hardships Oliver had to go through on the road before he reached Barnet.
e. Describe the odd-looking boy who met Oliver. What was his name?

II. Who said the following to whom?

a. "Been walking for seven days."
b. "Hello, my friend, what are you doing here?"
c. "I am very hungry and tired."
d. "What about a place to sleep?"
e. "I know an old gentleman who will provide you with a place to stay..."

III. Use the following words from the chapter in sentences of your own.

a. Undertaker
b. Milestone
c. Determination
d. Doorstep
e. Odd-looking

IV. In your own words describe the Artful Dodger. Would you like to have someone like the Artful Dodger as your friend?

Chapter 7

I. Answer the following questions.

a. Describe what Oliver saw when he was led into the dark room.
b. What explanation did Fagin give for the handkerchiefs on the line?
c. Who were the two visitors who entered the room? Describe them.
d. Why did Fagin say that he was proud of Oliver?
e. What explanation did the old gentlemen give the magistrate?
f. Why did the magistrate finally set Oliver free?

II. "Convinced that Oliver was still fast asleep, he locked the door and took out a box from a trap in the floorboard."

With reference to the above sentence answer the following questions.

a. Describe the contents of the box.
b. What did Fagin discover about Oliver when he looked up after examining the contents of the box?
c. What did Fagin run towards Oliver with?
d. What made Fagin calm down?
e. When did the box disappear?

III. In your own words, describe the strange game that Fagin and the boys played. What did you think about the game when you read the chapter?

Chapter 8

I. Answer the following questions.

a. Describe Oliver's condition for the first few days after he was taken to Mr. Brownlow's home.

b. Who cared for him during that time? Give a short character sketch of the person.

c. What did Oliver think about the soup?

d. What was Mr. Brownlow happy and unhappy to see about Oliver?

e. What did Mr. Brownlow think Oliver's name actually was? Why was Oliver worried about it?

II. "It was the first time in his life Oliver had ever experienced any kindness." Explain the reason why Oliver felt that way.

III. "As he enjoyed his meal he kept staring at a painting on the wall."
With reference to the above sentence answer the following questions.

a. What did Oliver ask Mrs. Bedwin about the painting?

b. What was her reply?

c. What were Oliver's feelings about the painting?

d. Later, what was Mr. Brownlow's reaction to seeing Oliver and the painting?

e. What did he point out to Mrs. Bedwin?

Chapter 9

I. Answer the following questions.

a. Describe Fagin's reaction when he heard about what had happened to Oliver.

b. What did he do to the Dodger in his anger?

c. Describe Bill Sikes.

d. What did Fagin and Bill want Nancy to do?

e. What was Fagin's reaction when Nancy gave him the news of what had happened to Oliver?

II. "Nancy, now looking very presentable, made her way towards the courthouse."
With reference to the above sentence answer the following questions.

a. What made Nancy look very presentable?

b. What did she call out when she reached the courtroom?

c. Whom did she question about seeing Oliver in the courtroom?

d. Whom did the clerk say had taken Oliver away?

e. What information did the clerk give Nancy about Oliver?

III. Find the meaning of the following words and phrases, and use them in sentences of your own:

a. Partner in crime
b. Disguised
c. Presentable
d. Precious
d. Desperate

Chapter 10

I. Answer the following questions.

a. What was the reason Mrs. Bedwin gave for the disappearance of the painting?

b. Was Oliver really happy in his new home? What makes you think so?

c. Why was Oliver worried when Mr. Brownlow sent for him?

d. What did Oliver beg of Mr. Brownlow?

e. Who was the visitor? Describe him.

II. "Oh, my dearest brother, I've finally found you."

With reference to the above sentence answer the following questions.

a. Who is the speaker?

b. Who was she referring to as her dearest brother?

c. What did she do next?

d. What did the speaker say to all the passersby?

e. Who came along and grabbed Oliver?

III. Fill in the blanks.

a. When Oliver entered the study, he found Mr. Brownlow reading a ______.

b. Mr. Brownlow handed ______ over to Oliver.

c. As Oliver walked along, towards the ______ thinking how blessed he was, he was startled by a young woman.

d. Oliver had broken his ______ heart yet preferred to stay with his new friends who were a pack of ______.

e. At that moment, Bill Sikes suddenly came forward along with his ______.

Chapter 11

I. Answer the following questions.

a. Why did Mrs. Bedwin not leave the door?

b. What was Mr. Bumble surprised to see while going through the newspaper?

c. Describe what happened when Mr. Bumble knocked on Mr. Brownlow's door.

d. What did Mr. Bumble tell Mr. Brownlow about Oliver?

e. What was Mr. Brownlow's reaction to the information given to him by Mr. Bumble?

II. "Mr. Brownlow was sad and disheartened to hear the story." Do you think

Mr. Brownlow was right in feeling that way? Why?

III. Use the following words from the chapter in sentences of your own.

a. Tormenting
b. Growled
c. Desperate
d. Echoed
e. Argument

IV. Shillings and pounds are the currency of which country? Can you find out the currencies of five different countries and list them down?

Chapter 12

I. Answer the following questions.

a. How did Sikes torment Oliver?
b. What did Fagin say to Oliver about his clothes?
c. What happened to the money that Dodger found with Oliver?
d. How did Oliver try to escape to his freedom?
e. What caused Nancy to faint?

II. Who said the following to whom?

a. "I'm so happy to see you again, Oliver, my dear."
b. "Give us the money right now, you lazy old Jew!"
c. "Hold back that dog, it will kill the boy!"
d. "Aren't you satisfied you have him back?"
e. "We better take off his best clothes too."

III. Do you think Nancy was a good person? What are the qualities she portrays in this chapter?

Chapter 13

I. Answer the following questions.

a. What did Fagin tell Oliver happened to boys who were ungrateful and spoke to the police?
b. Where did Fagin go after he locked Oliver up?
c. Who, according to Fagin, was the perfect candidate for the robbery? Why?
d. They finally stopped at a solitary, dilapidated house. Give any two incidents that happened next.
e. How did Oliver get into the room?

II. Name the following.

a. Sikes picked this up from the table and asked Oliver if he had seen something like this before. _______

b. Occasionally, Sikes would ask them to give Oliver and him a lift. ________

c. The man in the dilapidated house who was smoking a pipe. ______

d. The things taken along in preparation for the robbery. _______

e. Knowing they were being pursued, the thing Sikes dropped over Oliver because he was hit, before he left. _______

III. Oliver had decided that whether he survived or not he would warn the family in the house about the robbery. Do you think it was the right decision? Why?

Chapter 14

I. Answer the following questions.

a. Who visited Mrs. Corney, the matron who was in charge of the workhouse?

b. Why was Mrs. Corney in such a shock that she was about to scream?

c. What did the old woman who knocked on the door want from Mrs. Corney?

d. Where did the old woman take Mrs. Corney?

e. Who was the sick lady and what did she whisper to Mrs. Corney?

II. Find out the meanings of the following phrases used in the chapter and use them in sentences of your own.

a. Cheeks turn pink

b. Lost her voice

c. So distressed

d. In such shock

e. Watching over

III. The marriage contract was solemnly marked with a cup of tea. Can you think of different ways in which marriage contracts are marked today? (Hint: an engagement)

Chapter 15

I. Answer the following questions.

a. Who visited Fagin when he was sitting in his room and brooding?

b. What did Crackit tell Fagin of what he knew about the robbery?

c. On hearing the news from Crackit, where did Fagin go? Who was he planning to meet there?

d. After leaving The Three Cripples where did Fagin go?

e. All of a sudden Monks cried, "Look!" What had he seen?

II. State whether the following sentences are true or false.

a. The Dodger and Bill Sikes were in the room with Fagin when the bell rang. True/False

b. The man with his face covered with a scarf who entered the room was Toby Crackit. True/False

c. The robbery was a great success. True/False

d. The inside of The Three Cripples was dark and full of smoke and so it was impossible to see anyone clearly. True/False

e. When Fagin questioned Nancy about Sikes, she said she knew where he was. True/False

III. What is a "public house"? Do you think the name "Three Cripples" is a good name for a public house or for a hotel or any public place? Why?

Chapter 16

I. Answer the following questions.

a. When Oliver awoke, where did he find himself? What was his condition at that time?

b. Oliver staggered towards a house. What did he suddenly remember about the house?

c. What was happening inside the house when Oliver knocked on the door?

d. Who was Rose Maylie? Why were Rose and Mrs. Maylie shocked when they saw the thief?

e. "I have been an ungrateful boy, once," said Oliver. How had he been ungrateful?

II. "Oliver was well again and Dr. Losberne drove him to the place where Mr. Brownlow resided."

a. With reference to the above sentence answer the following questions.

b. How did Dr. Losberne and Oliver go to the place?

c. Did Oliver remember the house? Describe the house.

d. What did they discover when they reached the house?

e. What did they learn from the neighbors?

f. Why was Oliver disappointed?

III. "Within a fortnight, Mrs. Maylie and Rose took Oliver with them to the country to spend the summer there."
With reference to the above sentence answer the following questions.

a. What did Oliver enjoy about the countryside?

b. How did he spend his mornings?

c. What was the errand that Oliver had to run when Rose fell sick in the countryside?

d. Whom did he meet on returning from the doctor?

e. In a few lines describe what happened when Oliver was sitting at his window in his room one day.

Chapter 17

I. Answer the following questions.

a. The man handed two gold coins to Mr. Bumble for some information. What was the information that he wanted from him?

b. What was Sally holding on to when she died? Why was this item of importance?

c. Describe the contents of the small leather bag given to Monks by Mrs. Bumble.

d. Why was Bill Sikes angry with Fagin?

e. What did Nancy do when she left the room?

II. Who said the following to whom?

a. "Yes, just recently, to the workhouse matron."

b. "You mean something about the mother of the boy?"

c. "But what if I'm paying you for nothing?"

d. "Don't be frightened, look down."

e. "I think it's better that you take Nancy with you to fetch it."

III. Who is a pawnbroker? What is meant by a pawnbroker's duplicate?

Chapter 18

I. Answer the following questions.

a. When it was time for Sikes to go to bed, what did Nancy do?

b. What are the two qualities of Nancy mentioned in this chapter? Do you agree that she had these qualities in her?

c. How was Nancy to meet Rose again?

d. Describe the meeting between Oliver and Mr. Brownlow.

e. What do you know about the couple that was traveling along the road to London?

II. "The maid was not very happy with the way Nancy was dressed in shabby clothes." Do you think the maid was right in behaving the way she did? Why?

III. Use the following words from the chapter in sentences of your own.

a. Drug
b. Scarf
c. Smartly
d. Humanity
e. Information

IV. "If only there were more people like you in the world, there would be fewer people like me." Explain in your own words what you think Nancy meant by making this statement.

Chapter 19

I. Answer the following questions.

a. What was the news that Charley Bates brought with him?
b. How did Noah recognize the Dodger?
c. Why did the crowd cheer and laugh?
d. What did Sikes do to prevent Nancy from going out into the dark night?
e. What was the next mission Fagin wanted to send Noah on?

II. "A policeman stepped forward and explained how he had seen the boy try to pick the pocket of a gentleman."

Find out the importance of a handkerchief in those times. (Hint: made from silk). Would a pickpocket attempt to steal a handkerchief today? Why? What are the things pickpockets steal today?

III. "A large crowd had already collected at the courtroom. Most of them were women." Have you seen a courtroom? What does it look like? Who are the people who you see standing outside a courtroom? Is it the same scene as when the Dodger was in the courtroom?

Chapter 20

I. Answer the following questions.

a. Where was Nancy going?
b. What was the sound that Nancy heard? Whom did she see? Who were they?
c. What was the information about Monks that Nancy gave the couple?
d. Bill Sikes ran through the streets of London straight to his house. Mention any two of his actions after he entered the house.
e. "The shadow of death that had been following her now possessed her." Explain the line.

II. Who said the following to whom?

a. "Does he have any scars?"
b. "But, will you take this moneyat least?"
c. "Hell's fire!"
d. "Please, don't be too violent with her."
e. "Then please, spare my life."

III. Did Nancy betray Fagin? Which lines in the chapter tell you the same? Mention any two qualities of Nancy that you see in this chapter.

Chapter 21

I. Answer the following questions.

a. Mention all the people who stepped out of the carriage.

b. What were the threats Mr. Brownlow gave Monks?

c. Why was Mr. Brownlow being kind to Monks? What was Monks' real name?

d. Why did Monks' father travel to Rome?

e. What did Monks' father tell Mr. Brownlow?

f. On what condition would Monks be set free?

I. Find the meanings of the following words and phrases from the chapter and use them in sentences of your own.

a. Inheritance | b. Escorted

c. Lift a finger | d. Was shattered

e. Like a miracle

II. Where are the West Indies? How did people travel to the West Indies in the days of Oliver Twist? How can you travel to the West Indies today?

Chapter 22

. Answer the following questions.

a. What do you know about Jacob's Tavern?

b. Who suddenly bolted into the tavern? What did this mean?

c. A tapping was heard on the door. Describe the person who had arrived.

d. How did Charley behave when he saw Sikes? Mention any two of his reactions.

e. Why did Crackit point to the window?

. "I saw the tide was in as I came upstairs." What do you know about tides? How many types of tides are there? How would the tide help Sikes escape to freedom? Did it actually help him?

I. In your own words describe Sikes' end.

Chapter 23

Answer the following questions.

a. What was the request made by Oliver to Rose regarding his friend Dick?

b. Where did the coach finally stop? What did Oliver remember about the place?

c. How did Mr. Brownlow introduce Monks to Oliver?

d. What did the will of Monks' father state?

e. Describe Mr. Bumble's reaction when he saw Oliver.

. "Mr. Brownlow was now at the end of his revelations." With reference to the above sentence answer the following questions.

a. What did Mr. Brownlow say to Rose?

b. How did Mr. Brownlow explain to them who Rose was?

c. What did Monks' mother do when she found Agnes' sister?

d. What was Rose's reaction to the news?

e. How did Mrs. Maylie console her?

III. What is a will? Find out details about who makes a will and any two uses of a will.

Chapter 24

I. Answer the following questions.

a. Describe Fagin standing in the courtroom.

b. Mention any one thing Fagin thought of as he sat on the stone bench in his cell.

c. What does the clock striking signify to most people? What did it signify to Fagin?

d. Who were the two visitors who came to see Fagin on the day he was to be hanged? Why was the man on duty concerned to see one of the visitors?

e. What did one of the visitors want from Fagin?

II. "Mr. Brownlow hesitated to let Oliver go towards this crazy man." Do you think he did the right thing by allowing Oliver to go to Fagin? What qualities do you see in Oliver when he agreed to go to Fagin?

III. Who said the following to whom?

a. "Why couldn't they put in a light?"

b. "Is the young gentleman with you also going to see the prisoner, sir?"

c. "Let me whisper to you where the papers are."

d. "I am not frightened of him."

e. "Take me with you, now!"

IV. "Forgive this wretched man!"

What would your reaction have been were you in Oliver's place at this moment? Write a line about the importance of forgiveness.

Chapter 25

I. The story finally had a happy ending, not only for Oliver but also for most of the other characters. Write a line about what happened to each of the following.

a. Rose

b. Mrs. Maylie

c. Monks

d. Mr. Brownlow

e. Oliver

f. Noah Claypole

g. Mr. and Mrs. Bumble